The Little Vampire Moves In

Angela Sommer-Bodenburg

Illustrated by Amelie Glienke

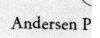

Andersen P

D1197849

Anderson Press Limited,
20 Vauxhall Bridge Road, London SW1V 2SA
www.andersenpress.co.uk

This edition first published in 2006

Reprinted 2008

British Library Cataloguing in Publication Data available
ISBN 978 1 84270 596 4

Printed and bound in Great Britain by
CPI Bookmarque, Croydon, CR0 4TD

Contents

*This book is especially for Katja,
who played with her cuddly animals
all the time I sat at my desk—
and for everybody whose vampire-
fangs have already grown, and for
those, like Burghardt Bodenburg,
who are still waiting for them.*

Angela Sommer-Bodenburg

1
A Fright in the Bath

Tony was lying in his bath, reading *In the House of Count Dracula,* when the front door bell rang.

'Hope it's not for me!' he thought, looking up from his book. He heard his mother open the door, and then come back across the hall to the bathroom, where she knocked.

'Someone to see you.'

'I'm reading,' grumbled Tony. 'Who is it?'

'A vampire.'

'A vampire?' exclaimed Tony. He was so startled he nearly dropped his book in the water! But on second thoughts, his mother must be being sarcastic, because *she* did not believe in vampires, even though she had recently met two of them! Both she and Tony's father believed that the two characters with their mouldering, smelly vampire-cloaks were simply a couple of children who had delved a little too deeply into their grandmother's dressing-up box. So he merely asked cautiously: 'Which vampire is it?'

'Rudolph,' came the answer.

That gave Tony another fright. Something terrible must have happened to make Rudolph come to him at the flat!

'Just a minute, I'm coming,' he called, clambering out of the bath.

In the hallway stood the little vampire. He looked grey and hollow-cheeked, and his little red eyes flickered feverishly.

'I must talk to you,' he whispered.

Tony gulped. 'Here?' he asked incredulously, looking over at the living room where his parents were sitting.

The little vampire looked at him imploringly. 'You *must* help me!' he whispered. 'You're my only friend!'

'I am? Oh. Well, er, how—?' stuttered Tony.

'Come down to the basement as soon as you can.' With these words, the little vampire turned around and disappeared.

'Has he gone already?' called Tony's mother. 'I was just getting some squash for you.'

'He doesn't like it,' said Tony, who was preoccupied with other thoughts. How on earth was he going to get away with going down to the basement at this time of the evening?

While he was getting dressed, he announced casually: 'I'm just going downstairs.'

'What? Now?' exclaimed his mother. 'Your hair's all wet—Has this got something to do with your funny friend?' she asked suspiciously.

'No,' lied Tony.

'Why do you need to go out then?'

'To bring in my bike.'

'Your new bike?' Dad's voice joined in now. 'Do you mean you left it outside, and all this time you've been lying about in the bath?'

'Yes.' Tony hid a smile, knowing quite well that his bicycle had been safely locked indoors for the past two hours. 'I'll be right back.'

Grinning, he shut the front door behind him and pressed the lift call button. What a fuss about a lousy bike! All he needed now was for Dad to call after him, 'Don't forget to lock up!' The lift arrived and Tony got in. On the way down, he remembered how exhausted and depressed the little vampire had seemed. His high spirits dwindled. What could have happened to make Rudolph come to the flat for help? What if the Nightwatchman had discovered the vault, and Rudolph was the only survivor? Tony's heart began to beat more quickly: that would mean that Anna, Rudolph's little sister . . . . No! Vampires were not beaten that easily, and especially not by old McRookery, although he was by no means

9

harmless—Rudolph had already told him of McRookery's ambition to have the first vampire-free cemetery in Europe! By this time, Tony had reached the basement. He opened the door of the lift and listened—not a sound! Cautiously, he took a couple of steps, then switched on the light. The basement corridor was empty, the door to the bicycle lockers shut.

Slowly he moved forward till he came to the door. He stopped and listened again. Nothing to be heard. He took a deep breath and turned the handle. At once, he was met by a familiar smell: a dank smell of coffins and decay!

'Rudolph?' he called hesitantly.

'Psst!' It came from the darkness. 'Come in and shut the door!'

2
Banishment

Just before Tony shut the door behind him, the light from the basement corridor revealed not only the bicycles leaning against one wall, but also a large box, on which were sitting two shadowy figures. Then everything went dark, and it took a couple of minutes before Tony's eyes adjusted themselves to the pale light which filtered through the two tiny windows. Now he could see that the two figures were wearing cloaks and that their faces were pale and ghostly. So both were vampires! The smaller, slighter one could only be Rudolph—but who might the second stronger and bigger one be?

'Rudolph?' said Tony uncertainly.

'Yes!' came the reply. 'Why don't you come and sit down?'

'Where?'

'Here, on the coffin with us!'

'Coffin?' So the large box was a coffin! A terrible thought occurred to Tony: supposing the coffin were for him? He'd read often enough how ordinary people were turned into vampires . . . .

'Come on!' called Rudolph impatiently.

Knees knocking, Tony groped his way over to the coffin and sat down on the very edge.

'Is something bothering you?' laughed Rudolph.

'I—er . . . .'

'He's scared!' The second figure spoke, and the grating voice sounded familiar. 'He doesn't know what to expect!'

'I ought to be getting back!' said Tony hastily.

'Did you say where you were going?' asked Rudolph sharply.

'N-no,' stammered Tony.

'Good.' Rudolph sounded relaxed once more. 'I'll tell you what all this is about.' He paused and listened. Tony tried to get a look at the second vampire, but could not be sure who it was.

'Listen!' Although all was quiet, Rudolph's voice sank to a whisper. 'I've left home. I've been banished from the vault.'

'Banished?' Tony did not understand.

'Yes. I'm not allowed back there any more.'

'Why?'

'Because I've made friends with humans. That's strictly forbidden for vampires.'

'How did they find out?'

'From Aunt Dorothy. She's been sniffing about on my trail for weeks. She put the whole matter before the family council and they've forbidden me to go back to the vault.'

'How rotten!' exclaimed Tony angrily. 'Where are you going to live?'

Rudolph gave a little cough and said, 'Well, here, with you, I hope.'

'With *me*?' Tony was horrified. 'How on earth do you think you can do that? My parents . . . .'

'Oh, I don't mean in the flat,' interrupted Rudolph. 'I mean down here, in the basement.'

'But anyone can come in here!' Tony threw a despairing look at all the bicycles propped against the wall. 'People leave their bikes down here.'

12

Rudolph gestured impatiently. 'Not right here. I mean in the lock-up storeroom belonging to your flat.'

'You can't!' Tony was beside himself. 'Mum and Dad would find out at once!'

'No they wouldn't. Not if you were clever,' said the second vampire.

'What if Mum needs something from down here, like wine?'

'You'll have to fetch it for her!' came the croaking reply.

'And if Dad wants to do some carpentry?'

'Distract him! Put the telly on, or buy him a sports magazine!'

'Dad doesn't like sports magazines,' said Tony.

'He wouldn't! Well, you'll just have to think of something else. You're not that stupid.'

'O.K., O.K.,' said Tony quickly to avoid rubbing him up the wrong way any further. Perhaps he was Gruesome Gregory, Rudolph's elder brother? He was just as bad-tempered as this, and Tony got the jitters whenever he thought of him.

'What about the coffin? You're not thinking of keeping that here too?' he asked.

'That's the most important thing! Where else would I sleep?' exclaimed Rudolph. 'Or did you think we'd lumped it all the way here just for fun?'

'Oh, er, no, of course not—it's just that the storeroom's a bit full and . . . .'

'We'll just have to make room for it then,' declared Rudolph, and stood up. The second vampire slid off the coffin too.

'What are we waiting for?' he growled.

'I–I haven't got the key!' said Tony. 'It's upstairs. I didn't realise . . . .'

'Well, go and get it!' ordered the larger vampire. 'And hurry up!'

'O.K.,' said Tony, stumbling to the door.

Tony ran through the basement and up the steps to the lift. What reason could he give his parents for having to go back down to the basement again? Perhaps he could simply try to creep in and out of the flat unnoticed? But he'd already been out for far too long, and if he didn't show up soon, they'd be bound to come downstairs looking for him. He'd better start thinking up some story. He felt better once this was decided, and took the lift up to his floor.

'Tony?' called his mother as he unlocked the door.

'Yes?' he answered, in his most cheery voice.

'Come here at once. Why have you been out so long?'

'I–er, I met someone from school down there.'

'Oh yes?' said Dad scornfully. 'In the basement I suppose?'

'No, of course not. On the stairs.'

'Who was it?' asked Mum.

'Andrew.'

'I thought you didn't like him?'

'Oh yes I do,' said Tony decisively. 'What's more, he's asked me to go and have a game of monopoly with him. Can I take my board down?'

'Now?' exclaimed Mum.

'It's only just after seven!' pleaded Tony. He was

thinking of the vampires, who had already been waiting for him for ten minutes. And if the second vampire *was* Gregory, there would be a terrible row if he kept them waiting for much longer.

'Funny to invite you and then ask *you* to bring the game along,' remarked Dad.

'Not really,' said Tony. 'He hasn't got one.'

'Where does this Andrew friend of yours live?' inquired Mum.

'On the, er, second floor.'

His mother held his gaze searchingly for a minute, then she relented. 'All right. But by eight, I want you back here in the flat.'

'Of course!' said Tony, and bit his tongue in an effort not to smile with relief. 'See you . . . .'

He tiptoed over to the hook with the keys hanging on it, took the storeroom key off it and slipped it into his pocket. He was already at the front door when his father called after him: 'What about the monopoly board?'

'Oh yes,' murmured Tony, 'of course.'

He ran to his room. Where had he last seen the board? On his table? Frantically he rummaged through his drawers. It wasn't on the bookshelf either, and in the cupboard he could only find stamp albums and comics. Finally, his glance fell on a compendium of games. That would have to do! He tucked the box under his arm and went out into the hall.

'See you later!' he called, and quickly shut the door behind him.

3
Coffin Bearers

'At last!' the larger vampire greeted him when he finally reached the basement. 'You took your time about it!'

'I–er, I had to tell my parents where I was going. I pretended I was going to see a friend.'

'Bah—friend!' spat the larger vampire. 'Come and give a hand with the coffin.'

'What about the game?' said Tony helplessly.

'What game?' The vampire surveyed the box under Tony's arm. 'Give it to me!' He snatched it away and hid it in the folds of his cloak.

'Hey!' protested Tony looking imploringly at Rudolph. But the little vampire only shrugged his shoulders.

'Now, let's get going!' growled the larger vampire. 'Take the handles—you at the front, Rudolph at the back.'

'What about you?' asked Tony, lifting the coffin.

'I'll hold the door open.'

The coffin was heavier than Tony had imagined—and Rudolph was not the strongest of carriers! With aching muscles, they reached the door of the storeroom.

'Well?' grinned the larger vampire, watching Tony and Rudolph rubbing their stinging fingers.

'How on earth did you get it all the way here?' asked Tony.

'Greg carried it,' replied Rudolph.

'By myself, what's more!' boasted Greg.

17

'I see,' murmured Tony. So it *was* Gruesome Gregory. He looked at him respectfully: it could certainly be highly dangerous to get on the wrong side of *him*!

'Aren't you going to open up?' growled Greg.

'Of course,' answered Tony hastily, fumbling in his pocket for the key. With trembling hands, he turned the lock and the door creaked open. Greg pushed the coffin inside and shut the door behind them.

'Sh–shall I put on the light?' quavered Tony.

'Light?' snorted Greg. 'Are you mad?'

'But you can't see anything!'

'I can,' declared Greg, and began to push to one side all the cardboard boxes which stood in the middle of the floor.

'Careful!' cried Tony. 'Those are bottles of wine!' But it was too late—there was the tinkle of broken glass and a large puddle began to form on the floor.

'Doesn't matter!' blustered Greg. 'It'll dry out.'

'Where shall we put my coffin?' Rudolph wanted to know.

'At the back, amongst all the junk,' said Greg.

There was an indignant protest from Rudolph. 'Why do I have to be put with the junk?'

'It'll be less noticeable that way,' explained Greg.

'B–but we haven't got any junk,' said Tony. 'Dad clears the storeroom out once a month.'

'That's great!' said Rudolph. 'Now you tell us! What if he finds me?'

'Tony'll know how to stop him,' said Greg, giving Tony an encouraging nudge in the shoulder, 'won't you?'

'Er, yeah,' muttered Tony, who was feeling more and more miserable at the thought of what the next weeks would bring. 'I–I'll pick up the bits of bottle.' He groped in one of the boxes and let out a cry. 'Ow, my finger!'

At once Greg's interest was aroused. 'Let me see—is there any blood?' he asked excitedly.

'Yes, er, I mean no,' said Tony, and quickly put his finger in his mouth. It was bleeding quite badly, but he said: 'It's stopped already.' Vampires and blood! He already knew that they fed on blood, and he had read somewhere that they could smell a drop of blood several metres away! 'Don't you think we should get on with stowing away the coffin?' he suggested. 'It's time I was getting back ....'

'That can wait,' said Greg. 'First I want to see your finger.'

'H–here,' stammered Tony. The cut was still there, but it had stopped bleeding.

Greg sniffed at each finger. 'Nothing!' he grumbled, turning away in disappointment. 'Come on! Let's get rid of this thing! I'm hungry.'

'Can't I switch the light on now?' asked Tony. If he didn't, who could tell what damage they might cause?

'O.K.,' growled Greg.

Tony switched on the light—and stood transfixed, his hair standing on end. Greg was a terrifying sight: white as chalk, with a gaping, scarlet mouth from the corners of which protruded two long, dangerous-looking teeth: the teeth of a beast of prey.

'What's up with you?' asked Greg. 'Gone on strike, have you?'

'N–no,' stuttered Tony.

'I'd like it to be behind that chest,' Rudolph decided.

'Sorry—you can't,' said Tony. 'That's got potatoes in it and it's nailed to the wall.'

'Well, next to it then.'

Greg pushed the coffin against the wall and looked around him. His eyes fell on a stack of wooden planks which Tony's father was going to use to face the kitchen wall.

'Those'll do nicely!' he announced.

He leaned them up against the wall of the storeroom so that the coffin lay hidden behind them. 'So, that's that,' he said. 'Now I must have something to eat before I die of hunger. You coming, Rudolph?'

Tony was on his toes at once, but Greg's hunger pangs did not seem to be directed at him, because he was standing at the window and had already pulled the grating aside. With one powerful leap, he sprang up and clambered through it. Rudolph followed.

'And leave the window open, understand?' hissed Greg, spreading out his arms under his cloak.

'O.K.,' said Tony. He heard the vampires fly off into the darkness, then all was quiet.

If only it was all just a dream, thought Tony. But there stood the planks against the wall, and behind them was the coffin.

Dejectedly he went to the door, flicked off the

light and pushed the catch down on the lock. The next few weeks were certainly going to pose some problems!

4
Gloomy Outlook

Tony's parents were still watching television.

'Well, how was it?' called Dad.

'Fine,' answered Tony, hoping to go on past the living-room door and into his bedroom. He was worn out!

'How was the game of monopoly?'

Tony stopped. 'Fine,' he said with a yawn.

'Did you bring it back?'

'Yes.'

'That's funny,' said Dad. 'I could have sworn you weren't carrying it when you walked past the door.'

'I've already put it back in my room.'

'I see. In that case, how do you explain that it's sitting here on top of the television?'

That brought Tony up with a start. 'Oh. I, er, couldn't find it earlier, so I took the compendium of games with me instead.'

'Where is it?'

'I left it behind by mistake.'

Dad snorted with impatience. 'Well, isn't that brilliant?' he said. 'If everyone was as careless as you with their things . . . .'

But at that moment, the news began, and at once Dad's face assumed a look of total absorption. With an exasperated gesture in Tony's direction, Dad indicated that the interview was over.

'May I go now?' Tony could hardly keep the anger out of his voice.

Dad did not answer, but Mum stood up and put

her arm round Tony's shoulders. 'Come on,' she said, and went out with him. Once in the hall she said: 'You know what Dad's like with his News Round-Up.'

'He squeezes me like you'd squeeze a lemon, and then acts like he's nothing better to do than watch the stupid news!' fumed Tony.

'He only wants to know what's going on in the world.'

'Huh!' Tony scoffed. 'No day's any different. There's always a war going on somewhere, and the politicians never get any further. He'd do better to take a bit more notice of what's going on around *him*!'

'What sort of things?' asked Mum with a smile.

'For a start, he could notice that I'm fed up with him, and that he takes more notice of the news than of us.'

'He's not always like that,' said Mum soothingly. 'He's going to make a start on covering the kitchen walls with that wood this weekend.'

'What?' exclaimed Tony. 'I thought he was going to wait until the holidays.'

'He was, but he's decided to start it this weekend.'

'I'll—I'll help him then,' said Tony hurriedly. There might still be a chance to keep Dad out of the basement!

'That would be kind of you,' said Mum. 'Sleep well, dear.'

'Goodnight,' murmured Tony.

Today is Tuesday, he thought as he lay in bed. That means three more days till Saturday. He'd have to talk to Rudolph tomorrow. Perhaps together they'd be able to think of a way out.

5
Early Morning Mood

The next day was dull and rainy. It was already beginning to get dark by six o'clock. Tony's father was never home before half past six, and Tony's mother was sitting in her room marking essays, a job from which she was 'on no account to be disturbed', she had told Tony.

It was therefore the ideal opportunity to visit Rudolph in the basement without being noticed. Quietly, Tony crept across the hall, took the key off the hook and closed the front door behind him.

He took the lift down to the basement. He did not meet anyone on the way, and the basement too was deserted. The smell of mould and decay struck his nostrils immediately—he had never noticed it before. Perhaps it was Rudolph? He stopped in front of the door marked 'Peasbody' and listened.

'Rudolph?' he whispered, and knocked on the door. 'It's me, Tony.'

No answer. Perhaps Rudolph had already gone out? But it was still too light for that. Vampires are not allowed to leave their coffins before sunset.

'Rudolph?' he repeated, a little more loudly.

Again, all was silent. Perhaps he had never come back to the basement, but had spent the night somewhere else? But no, that was not possible either, he had to sleep in his coffin.

Tony knocked again. When there was still no answer, he unlocked the door and went in. By the dim light, he could see that the window was still barred. Rudolph must be in his coffin.

Carefully, he inched round the planks of wood and studied the coffin which lay behind them. The lid was closed, and only the funny mouldy smell showed it was not empty. From inside there came a muffled groan, something bumped and thumped, and then the lid was raised slowly. Rudolph's ashen face emerged. His eyes were still shut, his mouth open in a gigantic yawn which revealed his powerful pointed canine teeth.

'Rudolph?' whispered Tony.

The little vampire gave a start. 'Who's there?' he croaked.

'M–me!' stuttered Tony.

'Oh, it's you,' said the vampire, sounding relieved. He stretched. 'Something up?'

'Yes. I mean, no,' dithered Tony. 'Dad wants the planks.'

The vampire yawned. 'Which planks?'

'These, of course,' said Tony, pointing to the pieces of wood. 'What's more, he keeps all his tools down here as well.'

The vampire heaved himself up onto the edge of his coffin and sighed. 'What's all this got to do with me?'

'Don't you see?' Tony's voice sounded too loud. 'When he comes down here, he'll find you!'

'Oh.' The vampire rubbed his eyes sleepily. 'All these problems before I've had breakfast!' he complained.

'We've got to think of something!' urged Tony.

'If only I weren't so tired!' whined the little

vampire. 'I can't think!'

'Today is Wednesday!' continued Tony anxiously. 'He wants to get the wood on Saturday.'

The vampire turned his head to the wall and sighed. 'I understand,' he said, 'but I just can't think on an empty stomach . . . and anyway, you've disturbed my morning routine!' Now he sounded cross. 'I always read for a bit before I get up.'

He lay back in his coffin with an injured look on his face and felt under his pillow for candles, matches and a book. Without looking at Tony again, he lit the candle, fixed it securely to the edge of his coffin and began to read. Tony could not believe his eyes. There was the vampire, in the middle of this crisis, calmly lying there reading *The Revenge of Dracula*!

Did he expect Tony to cope with the whole thing on his own? That was really a bit unfair—he had a nerve to think he could lie there and expect Tony to remove all the little problems and difficulties as they arose!

'You've got no idea about what friends are for!' said Tony angrily.

'Ssssh!' hissed the vampire. 'If anyone disturbs my reading, I fly into a terrible rage.'

Tony bit his lips with frustration. Now what? He looked around the storeroom and tried to think. Should he put the planks back where they were before? But then what could he use to cover the coffin? Why was their storerooom so blooming tidy? Everybody else had mounds of junk which he could have easily used to hide Rudolph. What if he threw a large sheet over the coffin? But then Dad would be sure to want to know what was underneath. No, it wouldn't work. The only way out was somehow to stop Dad from coming down here at all.

'I'm off now,' he said.

'Don't come so early next time,' was all he got for an answer. 'I'm never at my best first thing in the morning.'

'You can say that again!' growled Tony, as he left the room.

6
Poor Excuses

Saturday was the day that Tony liked to sleep on late. By the time he woke up at ten or half past, his parents had usually already had breakfast and had gone off shopping. Tony's plate would be left on the kitchen table with a roll, and a boiled egg under an egg cosy next to it.

But this particular Saturday morning, Tony woke up very early. He turned on the light and looked blearily around the room. Wasn't he in the basement, and Dad was about to open the lid of the coffin . . . ? It must have been only a dream, because here he was in bed wearing his pyjamas!

He looked at his clock. Quarter past seven! Even his parents would still be asleep. Tony drew the bedclothes up around his chin with a sigh. He was sure he would not go back to sleep again, he was far too on edge for that. Would his plan work? And what would happen if it didn't?

He took out his newest book, *Voices from the Vault*, and tried to read. But the Horror of the Depths described in the book seemed to him so similar to the Horror that was at this moment lying in the depths of his block of flats that he did not feel like reading about it, and he put the book aside.

Perhaps the best thing to do would be to go and make breakfast. He climbed out of bed and went to the bathroom. He studied his reflection in the mirror. He looked pale and ashen—like his parents sometimes did on a Sunday morning, after a particularly lengthy night out! He scrubbed his face with his flannel until his skin glowed. Then he dressed and went into the kitchen. He filled the coffee percolator, and put a saucepan of milk and a saucepan of water for the boiled eggs on the stove.

Next he laid the table, and tried to think what else he needed. Of course—some fresh bread rolls! He waited till the eggs were ready, then ran down to the baker and bought six rolls. Well, he thought, if this doesn't impress Mum and Dad, nothing will! He went over to their bedroom door and knocked.

'Yes?' mumbled Mum sleepily.

'Breakfast!' called Tony. A couple of minutes passed, then his mother appeared in the doorway.

'Have you really made breakfast?' she asked.

'Of course,' said Tony, as though it were nothing unusual. 'Hurry up, or the eggs will get cold.'

'O.K., we're coming,' said Mum. 'I'll just wake Dad. He ought to be up by now anyway, if he's going to get on with the kitchen.'

Tony shuddered. He'd almost forgotten!

'What's all this? Breakfast ready?' exclaimed Dad with undisguised astonishment when he saw the kitchen table. He sat down, took his egg out of its eggcup and shook it.

'Hard as a rock, I'll bet!' he teased.

Tony looked hurt. 'You don't believe I can even boil an egg!'

'What's the coffee like?' Dad asked Mum.

'Excellent,' said Mum.

'Hardly surprising,' grumbled Tony, 'the machine made it automatically.'

'Fresh bread rolls too!' Dad took one and bit into it. 'I really wouldn't recognise my own son any more.' After a pause, he looked at Tony searchingly. 'What's it all in aid of?' he asked. 'Have you been up to mischief?'

'Me? No, of course not,' retorted Tony indignantly.

'Bad marks for your homework?'

'No.'

Dad spread his roll with butter but never took his eyes off Tony. 'Something must be up,' he said.

Tony hesitated. 'I–I've lost the key to the basement,' he said at last.

'You've what?' shouted Dad. 'How am I supposed to get the wood and the tools?'

'I d–don't know,' mumbled Tony, trying his hardest to look ashamed.

'How did you lose it?'

'While I was out on my bike yesterday.'

'Didn't you look for it?'

'No,' said Tony. 'It was already dark.'

'Then you'll go and look for it now!' thundered Dad. 'How can you be so incompetent?'

'I'll go right away,' said Tony.

'Let him at least finish his breakfast in peace,' interrupted Mum. 'The key's not that important.'

'I'm not hungry any more,' said Tony. At the door, he paused. 'Are—are you going to begin working in any case?' he asked cautiously.

'How can I without any tools?' growled Dad. 'No, I'll wait for you.'

On his way down in the lift, Tony sang as loudly as

31

he could. He was filled with the sweetness of victory: his plan had worked! No one had guessed that the storeroom key was at that very moment safely in his trouser pocket! He'd come back with it in the afternoon, but by then it would be too late for Dad to make a start. Then this evening, his parents were going to the cinema—and tomorrow, his grandparents were coming for the day, so Dad wouldn't be able to do it then either. Still singing, Tony set off for his friend Olly's house, where he would play monopoly until the afternoon—with Olly's board, of course!

7
A Late Visitor

It was half past eight. Tony was lying on his bed listening to music. Not long before, his parents had left the flat in a rush, as always. As usual, Tony had asked: 'When will you be back?' and Dad had answered: 'About midnight, I expect.' That suited Tony perfectly. Probably his parents thought that he did not like being left on his own—which was true, on the whole, except of course when there was a good film on the television. And especially—he turned over and groped for the newspaper showing all the programmes—when there was a fantastic thriller on like tonight, with all his favourite stars in it.

Something knocked at the window. Startled, Tony lifted his head. He had not yet drawn the curtains, and he could make out the shape of a figure on the window-sill. Was it Rudolph? Or his sister Anna? He noticed how fast his heart had begun to beat.

The figure knocked again, and then he heard Rudolph's voice: 'Come on! Open up!'

He ran over to the window and opened it. With a single bound, the vampire landed in the room.

'Phew!' he gasped. 'She nearly got me!'

'Who?' asked Tony.

'Aunt Dorothy. She's spying around outside.'

'What?' cried Tony. 'Does she know I live here?'

'Of course,' said the vampire. Then he giggled. 'But she doesn't know *I* live here too!'

Tony had gone as white as a sheet. 'H–how did she

33

find out wh–where I live?'

'She always followed me before I was banned from the vault,' explained Rudolph.

Tony stared at him in disbelief. Hadn't the little vampire once said that Aunt Dorothy was the worst of the lot? Supposing one night she came and tapped at his window and he opened it unsuspectingly . . . .

'Wh–what does she want?' he stammered.

'To find out where my coffin is.' The vampire stared out into the darkness, rubbed his bony fingers and smiled. 'But this time I've been too clever for her!'

Tony was still trembling. It was a terrifying thought, that Aunt Dorothy was on the look-out for him.

'Will she come back?' he asked anxiously.

'Not tonight, that's for sure,' said the vampire.

'What about tomorrow?'

The vampire shrugged his shoulders. 'The main thing is that she doesn't find my coffin.'

Tony bit his lips in anger. 'You're the most self-centred person I've ever met!' he muttered.

'I'm not a person,' said the vampire haughtily.

'Vampire then,' hissed Tony. 'You're worse than a corpse, that's for sure. Friendship doesn't count for anything with you.'

But instead of being ashamed, the vampire looked very pleased with himself. 'I wish the others had heard you say that,' he smiled. 'They're always saying I'm too nice.'

Tony turned away angrily. The vampire did not seem bothered in the slightest by anything apart

34

from his own problems, and even the thought that his bloodthirsty Aunt Dorothy was on Tony's trail did not seem to disturb him in the least.

'Well, whatever else you are, you're certainly not a friend.'

'How can you say that?' exclaimed the vampire. 'I've come all the way here to take you to a Vampire Ball.'

'To a—what?' asked Tony.

'A Vampire Ball.' Rudolph proudly opened out his cloak and Tony could see he was wearing another underneath. 'Or are your parents at home?'

'No,' said Tony. 'But what *is* a Vampire Ball?'

The vampire waved airily. 'You'll have to find out for yourself.' Then, suddenly businesslike, he added, 'Come on. We must turn you into a vampire.'

Tony nearly cried out loud. He knew only too well from his books how people are turned into vampires! Involuntarily, his hand flew to his neck in protection, but the little vampire only smiled.

'Not like that,' he said. 'You must make yourself up.'

'Make myself up?' echoed Tony.

'Of course. Isn't there any babycream? Or lipstick?'

'Y–yes. In the bathroom.'

'Well, what are we waiting for?'

8
Tony's New Look

Once in the bathroom, the little vampire helped Tony on with the cloak. Then he took a step or two backwards and looked him up and down critically. 'That's no good. Your jeans are sticking out of the bottom,' he declared. 'No vampire wears jeans.'

'What do you wear?' asked Tony.

The vampire lifted his cloak so that Tony could see his black woolly tights. 'These,' he said. 'Hand-knitted.'

'I haven't got any tights,' murmured Tony.

'Haven't you?' asked the vampire. 'What do you wear in the winter?'

'Long underpants!' said Tony. 'They're white.'

'Yukkk!' exploded the vampire. 'I'll tell you what. I'll lend you mine.'

'Yours?' said Tony. He was shocked. To have to wear a vampire's vampirish tights was really the last straw. But the vampire had already started to take them off.

'I've got two pairs on anyway,' he said, 'because of the holes . . . .' He held the tights out to Tony, who took off his jeans and put them on the stool.

'I hope they're big enough,' he muttered, feeling down each leg with his toes.

'Should be,' said the vampire cheerfully. 'They're Greg's.'

That's great! thought Tony. Not only do I have to wear these revolting things, but I may get into trouble with Gregory about them as well. What was more, the wool was terribly tickly.

'P–perhaps it would be better if I stayed at home,' he suggested hesitantly, not wanting the little vampire to guess what he was thinking.

'You don't want to let an opportunity like this slip by, do you?' exclaimed Rudolph.

'N–no,' said Tony. 'I–it's just, well, how many vampires do you think will be there?'

'All of us! That's why we have to be dead certain we've disguised you properly.'

'*Dead* certain?' How do you mean?'

'Well, that no one recognises you and you don't arouse suspicion. Let's start with your hair.' He grabbed the brush and tousled Tony's hair with it so roughly that he yelped.

'Ow! Watch out, you're making a mess of the cloak!'

'How? Have you got dandruff?' laughed the little vampire. 'Well, that's great! The cloak looks really good and used. Let's get on to your face. Where's the babycream?'

'In the cupboard,' replied Tony, plucking at his hair which now stood out from his head like a wild feather duster.

The vampire found the babycream and he put a generous squirt on Tony's cheeks.

'Now rub it in!' he ordered.

'That's easier said than done,' grumbled Tony, trying to smear the glutinous white paste more evenly over his face.

'That'll do,' said the vampire. 'Now we just shake some powder over the top.' With that, he seized the tin of talcum powder and shook it liberally all over Tony's face. Poor Tony gasped for air, but the vampire rubbed his hands together delightedly and chortled: 'A real little killer! Now, where's the lipstick?'

'In the bottom drawer,' said Tony in a strangled voice.

The vampire undid the lipstick and looked at it ecstatically. 'Blood red!' he murmured, and held it under his nose and sniffed at it. His face darkened immediately, and he hissed with disappointment. 'Huh, it's sweet as sugar. Obviously no good to eat.'

He began to outline Tony's lips with swift, deft strokes. 'With or without a drop of blood?' he asked.

'What would you advise?'

'With,' said the vampire, and made a couple of red dots at the corner of Tony's mouth. 'It looks more realistic like that, at any rate for vampire kids. Or did you think our parents flew around after us in order to wipe our mouths?' He giggled at the thought. 'So, all that's left are the bags under your eyes.'

'More make-up?' asked Tony wretchedly. It was already hot enough under all the babycream.

'Of course. To make you look really dead. What can we use?'

'Eyebrow pencil?' suggested Tony. 'There, on the second shelf.'

The vampire took the pencil and made deep circles under Tony's eyes. 'No one would ever recognise you!' he said triumphantly.

'What if it comes off?' asked Tony.

'It won't,' said Rudolph. 'Just don't get too close

38

to anyone.'

'I won't!' said Tony emphatically, thinking of Aunt Dorothy and all the little vampire's other terrifying relations.

'There you are!' The little vampire stepped back, looking pleased. 'You can have a look.'

Tony's knees felt like jelly as he got up from the edge of the bath where he had been sitting and looked in the mirror. What he saw exceeded his wildest expectations: a grisly, chalk-white mask stared back at him, the blood-red mouth was drawn into a devilish grin and two eyes looked out furtively from deep-set sockets.

'That's n–not me!' he stuttered.

'Pleased?' The vampire grinned happily. 'No one will recognise you—not even Anna,' he added with a giggle.

'Is Anna going to be there?'

'Of course. She's expecting you.'

Tony cleared his throat to hide his embarrassment, and changed the subject. 'I've had a very tough time trying to keep Dad out of the basement,' he said.

'So what?' The little vampire sounded very unconcerned.

'I won't be able to keep him away next Saturday. Can't you go back to the vault before then?'

'We'll see,' said Rudolph. 'Perhaps there'll be news.'

'I hope so,' sighed Tony.

'Let's go then,' said the little vampire, moving over to the window.

'I–I don't think I can remember how to fly any more,' said Tony.

'Can't you?' smiled the vampire, giving Tony a friendly dig in the ribs. 'Just do what I do. I shut my eyes before I jump—it always helps.'

'Are you scared too?' asked Tony in amazement.

'Not any more,' said the vampire and sprang off the windowsill into the night.

'M–me neither!' said Tony, and shut his eyes—and flew!

9
The Flight to the Vale of Doom

A gentle wind swelled Tony's cloak and ruffled his tousled hair. He spread out his arms and found himself gliding.

'Come on,' said Rudolph tugging at his cloak. 'The Ball will have started by now.' He pumped his arms strongly and climbed higher. Tony had difficulty keeping up.

'Wait for me!' he called. 'I can't go so fast.' He looked down anxiously. The houses looked like toys, and his own room, in which he had left a light burning, was just a tiny bright square.

The vampire slowed down a little. 'No head for heights?' he grinned.

'Yes,' said Tony quickly, as the moonlight revealed Rudolph's scornful expression.

The vampire looked relieved. 'Just as well,' he said. 'We've got another thirty miles to fly.'

'As far as that!' exclaimed Tony.

'You didn't think that one hundred vampires could hold a get-together in the town?'

'One hundred?' Tony was scared again. 'Where do you meet?'

'In the ruins in the Vale of Doom.'

'Vale of Doom? Aren't there werewolves there?'

The little vampire smiled. 'You don't believe in those fairy-tales?'

'Well,' Tony defended himself, 'I believe in vampires, don't I?'

'What?' spat Rudolph. 'You dare lump vampires

41

in the same basket as werewolves?'

'No, no,' soothed Tony hastily. 'I only meant that most people don't believe in vampires or werewolves either.'

'Then they're stupid,' pronounced the little vampire scornfully. 'Of course there have never been such things as werewolves. They're a vampire invention.'

'A vampire invention?'

'Yes. It was the easiest way to keep nosy busybodies from snooping around our bodies.'

Tony looked so amazed that the vampire had to laugh. 'Our great, great, great, great, great grand-vampire, Elizabeth the Sweet-Toothed, thought it up. She did not like humans spying on the Vampire Balls.'

'Weren't people frightened of vampires then?'

'Oh yes. But they knew that vampires never eat or drink during their festivities.' Then he grinned. 'Vampires get that over and done with before the party starts!'

'How odd. At a human party, the food and drink is the most important part of the evening.'

The vampire shrugged deprecatingly. 'You humans have no idea how to behave,' he said.

Tony scratched his chin and thought for a moment. 'Does that mean that the vampires will have eaten tonight before they all meet at the ruins?'

'Of course.'

'I see.' Tony let out a great sigh of relief. 'I hadn't realized.' He was quite looking forward to the party now! 'So what was the werewolf idea?' he asked.

'Simple,' said the vampire. 'In those days, there were wolves everywhere. Elizabeth the Sweet-Toothed only had to spread the rumour that the wolves which lurked around the ruins were in fact evil men, who turned into ravening beasts after sunset. Soon no one came near the ruins any more, and the vampires could hold their festivities in peace.'

'Are there still wolves around?' asked Tony timidly.

'No,' laughed the vampire. 'But the Vale of Doom still has a bad reputation. Anyway, the vampires were responsible to a certain extent for the decline in the number of wolves over the years. You see, in times of hardship, famine especially . . . .'

Tony felt himself blanch. He did not like to be reminded of the vampires' grisly eating habits!

'Look!' exclaimed the vampire. 'There it is! The Vale of Doom.'

In the pale light of the moon they looked down on a group of shadowy ruins, which stood in a clearing, looking dismal and rather menacing. It was a rambling old building: only the outside walls of each side wing were still standing, although in contrast, the main block looked as if it was in fairly good condition, as far as Tony could see. 'It's so dark,' he whispered.

'Vampires don't need lights,' answered Rudolph, 'but there'll be candles in the main hall.'

He flew on purposefully to the main tower, and landed on one of the parapets.

'Here?' Tony was surprised. He had landed next

43

to the vampire and was looking anxiously towards a flight of crumbling steps which led to the inside of the tower.

'We always come in from above,' explained the vampire. 'At least, nearly always.' He jumped off the parapet and set off down the steps.

'Wait!' called Tony and, knees knocking, he went clambering down behind him.

10
A Suspicious Reception

At first there was still enough moonlight to show Tony where he should put his feet on the crumbling steps, but after the first bend in the stairs, it was pitch dark. Tony felt his way tentatively with his toes, and more than once he had to clutch onto the cold stone wall of the tower or he would have fallen. It seemed to last forever before a feeble glimmer of light appeared on a landing. There stood the little vampire. Tony looked around uneasily. Everything seemed to contribute to the atmosphere of gloom and eeriness: the stairs, rotten and crumbling, which led off deeper in the darkness; the glistening wet walls of the tower with all their clefts and crannies, in which hundreds of bats had their homes, he was sure; and the dark passageway leading into the centre of the ruins.

'Come along,' said Rudolph, taking him by the arm. 'We ought to go on.'

'Where?' hesitated Tony.

'To the Great Hall,' answered Rudolph. 'Can't you hear the music? That's Sabina the Sinister playing the organ.'

He set off down the corridor, taking Tony with him. By now Tony could hear the organ music too, slow and solemn like in church.

'Is that really Sabina the Sinister?'

'Oh yes. We vampires love music,' said Rudolph enthusiastically.

They came to a large, empty hall with the

moonlight shining through its broken windows. Pieces of masonry and broken glass littered the floor.

'We're almost there,' whispered Rudolph. His pale face had a look of excitement and his teeth clattered together in a most unnerving manner. An even larger hall opened up before them. Black shrouds were hanging at the window recesses, and black candles burned in the brackets on the walls.

'Here,' whispered the vampire, and at once a dark figure slid out from the shadow of the doorway and came over to them. It was a lean-looking vampire, with long scars on his face. He looked at them suspiciously, and hissed: 'Who are you?'

The little vampire made a bow. 'I am Rudolph Sackville-Bagg,' he said, 'and this . . .' gesturing towards Tony '. . . is a friend of mine.'

'A friend of yours? Is he a vampire?'

'But of course!'

'He looks human to me!'

The hair on Tony's neck prickled.

'He's foreign,' explained the little vampire. 'He comes from Italy.'

'Are there vampires in Italy?'

'Oh yes. There's a villa there, Matschimo or something, and it's full of them.'

'What's the family name?' pursued the lean vampire.

'The family name?' hedged Rudolph. 'It's Peasbodiori the Multitudinous.'

'Multitudinous?'

'Yes, there are so many of them, you see.'

'What about your friend. What's his name?'

'Antonio Peasbodiori the Melancholy.'

Tony grinned surreptitiously. Antonio Peasbodiori—that sounded much grander than Tony Peasbody!

'I don't know,' said the lean vampire indecisively. 'I've never heard of . . . .' He thought for a moment, then leaned forward and sniffed at Tony's cloak. His face brightened for the first time. 'Mmmm,' he sighed, 'genuine coffin!' He scrutinised Tony once more from head to foot, but in a slightly more friendly way. 'All right then,' he growled, 'you can go in.'

Tony and Rudolph exchanged relieved glances. Then, just as they were about to go on, the other vampire laid a heavy hand on Tony's shoulder.

'Just a moment.'

'Y–yes?' quavered Tony.

'What's the climate like in Italy?'

Tony was taken aback. 'It–it's n–nice!' he stammered.

'I might come and visit you some time,' said the vampire, letting his hand drop. 'My rheumatism never gets any better in all this damp!'

With these words, he took up his position again in the doorway, and looked good-humouredly beyond Rudolph and Tony into the Great Hall.

11
The Joys of Dancing

Tony stopped on the threshold and held his breath. The smell of decay was so overpowering that for a moment he thought he would have to leave. It was not only that, either: onions and rotten eggs were also much in evidence. The little vampire took long, deep breaths. 'Ah,' he sighed. 'How lovely it smells!'

Tony cleared his throat. 'A bit of fresh air would be nice,' he murmured.

'What?' snorted Rudolph. 'Fresh air? You'd be deserted by all true vampires!' Looking round furtively, he added: 'Don't let anyone hear you say things like that. You'll give yourself away! Anyway, there'll be the presentation of the Perfume Prize shortly.'

'Perfume Prize?' asked Tony.

'The prize for the vampire who smells the most.'

At that moment, the organ music started once more, and at once the vampires, who had been sitting at tables around the room, rose to their feet and made their way in pairs to the middle of the hall.

'Come on,' said Rudolph. 'Let's have a dance too.'

'U–us?' faltered Tony.

'Come *on*.' The little vampire hooked an arm through Tony's and led him onto the floor, flashing his terrible predator's grin and nodding affably to all sides. 'You be the girl,' he whispered. 'Put your hands on my shoulders, bend you head a little and gaze at me lovingly!'

'M–me?' stammered Tony. 'A girl?'

'Of course. That will be the least noticeable. All vampire children look alike.'

Tony gulped, but, glancing round at the many vampires who were already looking curiously in their direction, he decided that the best thing would be to follow Rudolph's instructions. He sank his head on his shoulder and looked dreamily at his feet, while Rudolph whirled him round in a circle till everything was dancing in front of his eyes.

'I feel dizzy,' he groaned, but Rudolph held him all the more firmly.

'You dance like a dream!' he breathed.

'Really?' Tony was embarrassed. Dancing was not his favourite occupation!

'Yes,' replied Rudolph. 'You ought to see Greg trying to dance!'

'What's that about me?' interrupted a hoarse voice. A tall vampire emerged from the throng and came up to them with slow, purposeful strides. It was Gruesome Gregory. Tony blanched. What if he recognised . . . ?

'Nothing,' said Rudolph hastily.

'You were talking about me,' accused Greg, his voice cracking.

'I only said: "There's Greg,"' said Rudolph, who could not think of a better explanation on the spur of the moment.

'Why?' growled Greg.

'Because . . . .' Rudolph looked helplessly at Tony. 'My friend here from Italy wanted your autograph.'

'My autograph?' Greg surveyed Tony carefully

from under lowered lids. 'Why mine?'

Rudolph gave an extravagant, Italian-like gesture. 'Why do you ask? Your reputation has spread . . . .'

'Really?' Greg was flattered. Swiftly, he turned away and disappeared among the dancers.

'Now my family will know I'm here,' murmured Rudolph. 'Greg will spread the news.'

'Does that matter?'

'We'll have to see. Admittedly, I was banned from the vault—but not banned from dancing!' he finished defiantly, took Tony round the waist once more and went on with the dance.

12
The First Kiss

'Tony?' Someone was plucking at his cloak, and he spun round in a fright.

'Anna!'

She lowered her eyes shyly. 'Greg told me you were here. Shall we dance?'

'Er—I'm . . . .' He looked helplessly from Anna to her brother. 'I've already got a partner.'

Anna giggled. 'Him?'

Rudolph stepped to one side. 'Please—don't let me stop you.'

Anna curtsied. 'Thank you,' she said, then added: 'In any case, I'd make myself scarce if I were you. If Aunt Dorothy sees you . . . .'

The little vampire shrugged his shoulders indifferently. 'So what? This isn't the vault!' he said, and turned away.

'Wh–where are you going?' called Tony anxiously, but Rudolph had disappeared. 'Thanks for abandoning me!' he muttered.

'You've got me!' laughed Anna throwing her arms around his neck and drawing close. Tony felt weak and faint—and it certainly was not only due to the smell in the air!

While they danced, he studied her furtively: she had closed her eyes and was humming softly to the music. Her tiny, red lips were smiling, and her cheeks were slightly pink, as if she were really alive. Only her tattered cloak reminded him that she was a vampire. But did she count as one? After all, she did

53

not have vampire fangs! She opened her eyes suddenly. 'Nice isn't it?' she whispered.

'Y–yes,' stammered Tony.

'What do you think of me?'

'Oh.' He gulped. 'I think you're, er, sweet.'

'Really?' Her blush deepened. 'Oh Tony.' She stood on tiptoe and kissed him on the lips.

Tony stood rooted to the spot. It seemed to him as though every vampire in the room must be staring at them. He couldn't believe that they were all dancing on as though nothing had happened.

'Are you cross with me?' asked Anna cautiously after a while.

'No,' muttered Tony, embarrassed.

She gave a sigh of relief. 'I'm so impetuous, you know,' she explained. 'Rudolph says I must learn to master my feelings better—a bit difficult, especially as I could only ever "mistress" them!' she added mischievously.

While she was speaking, Tony flicked his tongue rapidly over his lips. They felt dry and smooth, and there was certainly no trace of blood.

'How are you enjoying the party?' asked Anna.

Tony looked around uncertainly. 'It's a bit dreary, I think.'

'I agree,' nodded Anna. 'I wanted to put a disco in the dungeon, but the oldies wouldn't have it.' She looked up at the organ and made a face. 'It's always this oom-pah-pah,' she complained.

'We could always go outside for a breath of fresh air?' suggested Tony, whose head was reeling.

'Oh yes!' said Anna enthusiastically. 'Let's go for

a walk in the moonlight!' She took Tony's hand and drew him towards the doorway.

The two of them crossed the hall and reached a dark stairway. The great door stood ajar, and they went through it out into an overgrown garden. The grass grew knee-high, and shrubs and bushes had long since grown over the paths. Anna took Tony's hand and laid her head on his shoulder.

'My–my leg's gone to sleep,' said Tony loudly, who was finding Anna's increasing friendliness more and more alarming.

'I love moonlight nights,' said Anna dreamily. Then, in a slightly louder voice, she continued: 'Do you see the moon? We see but the half of it, and yet it is round and beautiful. Similarly, there are many things which we ridicule in our arrogance, because our eyes cannot perceive them.'

Tony glanced at her in surprise. 'Did you make that up?' he asked.

'No,' she laughed, 'but it's beautiful, isn't it? Moonlight always makes me sentimental.' She looked up at Tony with swimming eyes, and a tear rolled slowly down one cheek.

'Wh–why are you crying?' asked Tony.

'Because I'm so happy,' she whispered, and ran away.

'Anna!' called Tony in dismay.

Nobody answered. Only the hazel bushes rustled softly.

'Anna!' he called again.

This time a voice answered, 'Here I am!' Was that Anna's voice? It sounded rather muffled. A terrible

dread came over him. He stood still, indecisive, and held his breath.

'Where are you?' called the voice, and this time there was no doubt about it: it definitely was not Anna! Who could it be? He thought of the werewolves Rudolph had told him about . . . .

Something was gleaming among the bushes. Tony felt himself inexplicably drawn towards them, and nothing he could do could stop him from taking one, then two faltering steps in their direction. Then suddenly something grabbed him from behind.

'Tony!' A voice was calling him urgently. It was Anna! 'Quickly! Back to the hall! It's Aunt Dorothy over there . . . !'

Tony glimpsed a shadow emerge from the bushes and hurry closer and closer, but by then he and Anna had reached the door and closed it tightly behind them. Trembling from head to foot, Anna leaned against it. 'She nearly got you!' she whispered. 'And it would have been all my fault.'

'I thought she was inside,' said Tony.

'I thought so too,' said Anna quietly. Her lips quivered, and her face was as white as chalk. 'Tony, you must never go outside alone in the moonlight again.'

'No I won't!' Tony assured her.

'Shall we go back to the hall?'

'What about Aunt Dorothy?'

'She can't do anything indoors,' said Anna. 'That's why she wanted to fortify herself first.'

'You call that fortifying herself?' said Tony crossly, gingerly feeling his neck.

Anna laughed. 'Come on. Perhaps they'll be giving the Perfume Prize soon.'

13
Who Has the Best Smell?

The organ music had stopped by the time the two friends had reached the Great Hall. The vampires had returned to their tables, and all eyes were staring fixedly at a small, rather bowed vampire who was standing in the middle of the hall on a podium. 'Elizabeth the Sweet-Toothed,' whispered Anna, who had found two spare seats near the entrance.

Unlike most other vampires who seemed to pay little attention to their appearance, Elizabeth the Sweet-Toothed was very scrupulously dressed: she was wearing a spotless cloak of black silk, her grey hair was curled in tiny ringlets, and rings sparkled on her gnarled old fingers.

'My dear friends!' she began. 'It gives me great pleasure that you are all here tonight. The moment you have all been waiting for has now arrived: the judging of "The Perfume Prize". The judges this time are Magdalene the Double-Dealing, Good-Natured Gordon and Mabel the Mean. I call upon the judges to take their seats.'

The three vampires joined her on the podium.

'The one with the glasses is Magdalene,' whispered Anna. 'She thinks she's got the best legs of any vampire!'

'Really?' giggled Tony. Magdalene's cloak stopped at her knees, and from underneath protruded two short, stocky calves that were anything but elegant.

'Why is that one called Good-Natured Gordon?'

asked Tony.

'Can't you see how thin he is?' smiled Anna. 'He's so good-natured that he always lets other vampires go first.'

Mabel the Mean was taller than the other two vampires by a head. She was in pretty good shape for a vampire, thought Tony, but jealousy and greed had etched deep lines into her face.

'I now ask any vampire who wishes to enter this competition to step forward and wait in a line!' called out Elizabeth the Sweet-Toothed. At once, about ten vampires left their seats.

'Would the first competitor please come forward!'

A thick-set vampire with a completely round bald head stepped onto the podium. 'I am George the Boisterous,' he said in a grating voice. 'I have entered this competition because to my mind I smell truly spicy.'

'Let me smell you!' trilled Magdalene the Double-Dealing, and she began to sniff at him. The other two vampires followed suit. Then all three looked at one another and nodded.

'Next!' called Elizabeth the Sweet-Toothed.

This was a tall, lanky vampire. 'I am Hannah the Hasty,' she said in a high falsetto voice. 'My speciality is the fragrance of fresh horse manure.'

The judges all snuffled their way around her, and then came a bloated vampire with a double chin and little piggy eyes, a hollow-cheeked girl-vampire, a vampire with a patch over one eye, and an ancient vampire who could only speak in a whisper because all but his canine teeth were missing.

Then a tall, broad-shouldered vampire stepped
onto the podium. 'My name is Gruesome Gregory!'
he announced. 'I am famous for my aroma of decay.'

Anna clapped her hand over her mouth. 'Greg
doesn't have an aroma,' she murmured. 'It's more
like a stink!'

61

With an air of already having won the competition, Gregory strutted about the podium and allowed himself to be sniffed.

'He fancies himself,' hissed Anna.

After Gregory, two more vampires introduced themselves to the judges and the general gathering, and then the first part of the competition was over. Sabina the Sinister sat down at the organ again and played, while the judges went into a huddle with Elizabeth the Sweet-Toothed to come to a decision.

'Do you think Greg will win?' whispered Tony.

Anna shook her head. 'Never! I was sitting next to Hannah the Hasty earlier and Greg's got nothing on her! And who knows what the others smell like?'

At last, Elizabeth the Sweet-Toothed raised her arm, and abruptly the music stopped. 'My friends!' she announced in a stirring voice. 'The winner of tonight's competition, the vampire who smells the best, is —' she paused and looked down the row of waiting candidates, 'George the Boisterous!'

Thunderous applause broke out. George the Boisterous hobbled over to the podium and bowed.

'The prize tonight is a cuddly blanket for your coffin!' announced Elizabeth the Sweet-Toothed, handing over a piece of black cloth.

'Now Greg will be mad!' said Anna.

'But it was quite fair,' said Tony.

'Greg always thinks it's unfair when he doesn't win,' explained Anna, 'and it would be better if we didn't come across him. Let's go.'

'What about Rudolph?' asked Tony.

'He's gone home already by himself.'

14
Flying Home

'What if Aunt Dorothy catches me?' asked Tony as they stepped out onto the top platform of the tower.

'Oh,' said Anna shrugging carelessly, 'she's still lurking down there in the garden.' She soared up into the air and Tony spread his arms under his cloak and followed her.

'Fresh air!' he sighed and drew in deep breaths of it.

'What about my "Fragrant Earth"?' asked Anna peevishly. 'Can't you smell my perfume?'

'Yes, of course,' said Tony hastily. There was a certain unpleasant smell to be sure, but it did not bother him out here in the fresh air.

'I sprayed it on extra well tonight, just for you,' she declared.

'How nice of you,' murmured Tony.

'Do you really have to go home?' asked Anna, gazing at Tony with adoring eyes. 'We could do something else. I've always wanted to go to a disco, for instance.'

'Discos are boring,' declared Tony. 'They're a sheer waste of money!'

'We could go swimming then,' suggested Anna. 'A moonlight swim would be very romantic.'

'Er—I haven't got any bathing things with me,' Tony excused himself hastily.

'So what?' laughed Anna. 'Neither have I!'

'I've, er, got a cold,' said Tony, and sneezed to prove it.

'Huh!' grumbled Anna. 'You just don't want to go swimming.'

'My parents will be home soon,' said Tony. 'We must get back.'

'O.K.,' said Anna sadly.

For a while, they flew on in silence. Tony was angry with himself. He always seemed to make a mess of things.

'Shall I tell you a joke?' he asked finally.

'If you want,' replied Anna.

'Fred wanted to buy his dad a shirt for his birthday. "I'd like a smart shirt, please," he says to the salesman. "Like the one I am wearing, sir?" asks the salesman. "No," answers Fred, "a clean one!"'

'Ha, ha,' said Anna without smiling.

At least she's said something, thought Tony to himself. Feverishly, he tried to remember another joke he could tell her. 'There's this dog, a boxer, going for a walk down the street. Above him, two floors up, there's an alsatian on a balcony. "Jump down here!" calls the boxer. "We could go for a walk together." "Do you think I'm barmy?" answers the alsatian. "Do you think I want to end up with a nose like yours?"'

Anna could not stop herself smiling, but she still stared stonily in front of her.

'Do you know the one about the dachshund?' Tony continued. 'A man goes to the cinema with his dachshund. The dog laughs and laughs and won't stop. A lady turns round and comments: "That's a remarkable dog you have there." "Yes," replies the man, "I think he's odd too. Would you believe it, when I read the book of this film to him, he didn't laugh at all!"'

This time Anna laughed softly but surreptitiously. The ice was broken! Tony only had to make her laugh out loud, and he knew just the joke to do it.

'Two cows were grazing peacefully in a meadow. Suddenly one of them begins to shiver violently. "Are you ill?" asks the other one anxiously. "Oh no," her friend replies, "but here comes the milkmaid with the freezing cold hands!"'

This was too much for Anna, and she burst out laughing. Tony laughed too, and together they flew on, giggling and spluttering.

'I can't wait to tell Greg that one,' she said.

Tony looked flattered.

'Do you know any more?' Tony shook his head.

'I only know one,' said Anna. 'A woman goes to her doctor. "Doctor", she complains, "everytime I drink a cup of coffee, I get this terrible pain in my right eye." "I suggest you take the spoon out of the cup!" advises the doctor.'

'My tummy aches from all this laughing!' gasped Tony.

'Not so loud!' warned Anna. 'We've nearly reached the town.'

Just in front of them, the first houses were rising up in the darkness. Tony remembered he had something important to discuss with Anna.

'How long is Rudolph banned from the vault?'

She shrugged her shoulders. 'Two, three months. Whatever the family council decides.'

'That long!' cried Tony. That was awful! How was he supposed to keep his parents out of the basement for that long? 'He leaves everything to me!' he complained. 'Right now this minute, he's lazing in his coffin, reading vampire stories and expecting me to solve all the problems!'

'Typical Rudolph!' grinned Anna. 'But you're the one to blame for letting him use you.'

'What shall I do?' asked Tony. 'Just wait and see what happens when Dad finds him?'

'Of course not,' Anna replied, 'but you must make it clear to him that he can't stay in your basement for ever. The family council meets again next week, and perhaps the ban will be lifted. In any case, I'll put in a good word for him.'

'Are you on the family council?' asked Tony, surprised.

'Of course. You didn't think I'd let anyone else look after my interests?'

By now they had reached Tony's house. His desk lamp was still on in his room. Tony gave a sigh of relief—that meant his parents weren't home yet!

He landed on the window-sill and opened the window, which he had left on the latch.

'Goodnight, Anna,' he said.

'Goodnight, Tony,' she replied. 'Don't forget to take off your make-up.'

15
Chicken Fricassee

When Tony woke up the next morning, he was suffering from a quite remarkable headache, and when he tried to get out of bed, everything went black. He sat back on his bed and thought. Had he eaten or drunk anything the day before that could have disagreed with him? But he had not touched anything at the Vampire Ball, and all the food at home was quite all right.

Perhaps he simply had not slept for long enough? He looked at the clock. Eleven already! He must have had nearly eleven hours' sleep! Perhaps the events of last night had just been too much for him, or the smell in the Great Hall had gone to his head!

A gentle tap on the door aroused him. 'Tony, are you awake?' asked his mother.

'No,' he said, and quickly pulled the bedclothes over his head. He heard his bedroom door being opened, and then two hands appeared under the bedclothes and began to tickle him.

'No!' he pleaded. 'Stop!'

'Are you awake now?' asked his mother, sitting down on the edge of the bed and watching her son emerge from the bedclothes.

'What do you look like?' she gasped in horror.

'What do you mean?' asked Tony.

'Your eyes look all glued up, and your skin's gone stripy!'

'Has it?' mumbled Tony. Perhaps he had not cleaned himself up properly last night. His eyes had refused to stay open any longer as he stood in front of the bathroom mirror, so he had made do with a couple of wipes across his face with a wet flannel. He had not realised the stuff was so difficult to get off . . . .

'Get yourself washed as quickly as you can!' ordered Mum. 'Gran and Grandpa are coming for lunch at twelve.'

'Oh yes,' he remembered.

'What's for lunch?' he asked his father on the way to the bathroom.

'Your favourite: chicken fricassee.'

'And for pudding?'

'Home-made vanilla ice-cream.'

'Mmmm,' said Tony, licking his lips. They still tasted of lipstick!

Just before twelve, the doorbell rang. Tony had got himself washed and dressed—though not in his black linen trousers, despite his mother's protests. 'You know what Gran thinks . . .' she had said, but Tony had remained obstinate and had put on his jeans. Rudolph's stinking cloak and holey tights had been stuffed into a pillowcase and thrown to the very back of his cupboard.

Tony's grandmother was a small, round little lady. When she laughed, she revealed a set of perfectly even, pearly-white teeth. Tony had always been very impressed by Gran's teeth—until the time he went to spend the night with his grandparents, and had discovered the teeth in a toothmug the next morning!

Tony's grandfather was not much taller. Usually he wore corduroy trousers and a checked shirt, but today he had put on his best suit.

He unwrapped a bunch of tulips and held them out to Tony's mother. And as usual, he pressed a flat little package into Tony's hand—a thick bar of milk chocolate with hazelnuts!

'Not till after you've had your lunch,' warned Gran.

'Of course not,' said Tony.

His grandparents hung up their coats and then sat down to table in the living room.

'Tony's looking so healthy with those glowing cheeks,' remarked Gran.

Tony grinned. Not surprising, if she only knew how hard he'd been scrubbing his face with the flannel!

'But you're still wearing those dreadful "jeans"!' she scolded. 'Can't you wear a decent pair of trousers, at least on Sundays?'

'Oh Gran, everyone wears jeans!'

'Grandpa doesn't!' she retorted.

'Shall I dish up?' offered Dad.

'I'll have a leg please,' said Gran.

'What did you say you wanted? A leg?' laughed Tony.

Gran looked at him sternly. 'That's what it's called, young man.'

'*We* call it a drumstick!' declared Tony.

'Slice of breast for me, please,' requested Grandpa, and Tony tried not to smile. He quickly piled some rice on his plate and bent over it, as if he were about to eat. The laughter was bubbling up inside him and he could hardly breathe!

'Delicious!' enthused Grandpa. 'There's nothing I like better than a well-cooked slice of breast.'

Tony hiccuped.

'Tell me,' continued Grandpa, 'have you started on the kitchen yet?'

Tony's father, whose mouth was full of rice, could only shake his head. 'Tony lost the key to the basement store.'

'You didn't!' exclaimed Grandpa. 'How could you lose a thing like that?'

'I did find it again,' growled Tony.

'Don't speak with your mouth full,' Gran rebuked him.

'What will you do now?' asked Grandpa. 'When will you start?'

'I've got to go to a conference all next weekend, and the weekend after that I think I shall relax a bit.'

'Really?' Tony could not believe his ears. This was fantastic. But his relief was short-lived.

'I know what,' said Grandpa. 'Why not take a day off this coming week, and I'll come and give you a hand. What do you think of that?'

Tony's father looked surprised. 'Not a bad idea,' he said. 'Tony's not much help at jobs like this,' he added.

'I beg your pardon?' said Tony indignantly. 'I can fetch the wood and the tools out of the basement.'

'I'd rather do that myself,' said Dad. 'Or Grandpa could do it. Does Thursday suit you?'

'Yes,' nodded Grandpa.

70

'That's settled then!' Everyone looked pleased—except for Tony.

'Eat up, young man!' said Gran, who had noticed how pale Tony had become. 'This will make you big and strong!'

'Yes, yes,' muttered Tony, stirring his rice round his plate. His appetite had strangely disappeared!

16
Waiting for Dusk

'Aren't you going to gym?' asked Tony's mother on Monday afternoon, shortly before five o'clock.

'Yes, but it's later today. Not till six.'

'Why?'

'Why?' Tony had not yet thought up an excuse. 'The trainer has to go to the dentist,' he said.

'How strange, when he's meant to be coaching you lot.' Tony's mother shook her head disbelievingly. 'That means it'll be dark when you come home.'

'That doesn't matter,' said Tony. 'Olly'll be coming back with me.'

'Oh, all right then.' Mum went back to marking arithmetic books.

Tony went to his room and read a book till just before six. Then he took his sports bag out of the cupboard, emptied the pillowcase of Rudolph's things, and stuffed them in with his sports clothes.

Of course he wasn't going to gym tonight. That always happened between five and six o'clock. Tonight, he was going to be with Olly from six until quarter to seven, and then, as soon as it was dark, he would visit the little vampire in the basement.

'When are you coming back?' asked Mum, as he said goodbye.

'Just after seven,' he answered.

On the way back from Olly's house, Tony came, to his horror, face to face with Mrs Starling, a

72

neighbour from the fourth floor, who was known to all the children in the building as 'Mrs Tittle-Tattle'. As usual, she was wearing her revolting old overall, and on her head was a transparent nylon scarf which held together a mass of hair curlers.

'Well, well, if it ain't Tony,' she said, smiling ingratiatingly. 'Out and about so late? It's a wonder you're not afraid, all by yourself down 'ere.'

'No,' muttered Tony, trying to get past her.

But she took his arm in a tight grip and hissed: ''Ave you noticed 'ow it's begun to stink in that basement lately? We shouldn't put up with it!'

She paused, and gulped for breath. 'If it doesn't get no better, everyone'll 'ave to open up their storerooms so as we can find out where the stink's coming from.'

Tony was dismayed. 'C–can you make people do that?' he stuttered.

''Course!' she said, ''specially at times like these . . . .' With these words, she let go of his arm and stalked off up the stairs. 'Stinks like a pigsty down there, it does,' Tony heard her grumble.

He waited in the passageway till all was quiet. Then he crossed quietly to their storeroom door, and knocked and went in.

The smell of mould and decay certainly did seem more noticeable now—or was it simply that Mrs Starling had drawn his attention to it?

He waited by the door and blinked. 'Rudolph?' he called quietly. 'I've brought your things back.'

'Why have you come so early again?' was the only answer to come from the depths of the storeroom.

'Can I turn on the light?' asked Tony cautiously.

'No!' cried the little vampire. 'For Lucifer's sake, no electric light so soon after waking me up!'

A match burned up brightly, and Tony saw the little vampire light the candle by his coffin.

'I haven't cleaned my teeth yet,' he muttered, and pulled a red toothbrush with twisted bristles out of his coffin.

'You haven't got any water,' remarked Tony.

'So?' spat the little vampire. 'Why would I need water just to brush my gums? The things you humans think of,' he added, brushing round his mouth energetically.

Tony took the cloak and tights out of the sports

bag and put them on the edge of the coffin. The vampire did not seem to want to take any notice either of him, or of the clothes.

'Why are you cross?' asked Tony finally. 'Is it because of yesterday?'

'Yes.'

Tony thought for a moment. 'Because I danced with Anna?'

'No!' Although he had been so guarded up till that moment, the vampire now positively boiled. 'Because you just cleared off, and I was looking all over the ruins for you and ran straight into Aunt Dorothy's waiting arms!'

'Oh,' was all Tony could think of to say. He could quite understand Rudolph's fright. 'What happened?'

'She called Elizabeth the Sweet-Toothed, who is our Vampire-in-Chief, and she gave me a punishment, because she said it was pure insolence to come to the Vampire Ball when I had been banned from the vault. *I* didn't know that meant I'd been banned from the party as well,' he grumbled.

'Does that mean the ban from the vault hasn't been lifted?' asked Tony.

'Not only that—I've been forbidden to fly for two days as well!'

'What does that mean?' asked Tony, mystified.

'Well, er, that I have to catch my food on foot.'

'All I hear is forbidden to do this, forbidden to do that!' snorted Tony. 'Forbidden to go to the vault, forbidden to go to the party, forbidden to fly . . . it's dictatorship!'

75

The little vampire shrugged his shoulders sadly. 'What can I do about it?' he asked.

'Revolt!' said Tony.

But the little vampire only shook his head wearily. 'That might work with you humans, but with vampires it would lead to the most dire consequences'—his voice lowered—'I'd be forbidden to carry on as a vampire.'

Tony still did not quite understand.

'That would mean starving to death,' said the vampire in sepulchral tones.

Tony was speechless. The vampires seemed to have the most outrageous ways of bringing up their children. He could only thank his lucky stars he wasn't one. 'Can I help in any way?' he asked sympathetically.

The little vampire's eyes began to gleam. 'Would you really do that for me?' he asked, licking his lips.

Tony's heart nearly stopped beating. 'I–I didn't mean like that!' he stammered. 'I–I meant in some other way.'

Rudolph's expression drooped. 'How?' he grunted. 'Do you want to help me catch mice?'

'No,' said Tony hastily. He really did seem to have the knack of landing himself in hot water!

'I think I'd better get going,' said the vampire gloomily. 'Who knows how long it's going to take me to get supper tonight.' He blew out the candle and stood up.

'Good luck,' said Tony quietly. He suddenly felt very sorry for the vampire. He, Tony, could simply go upstairs and get a piece of cheese out of the fridge whenever he felt hungry.

'Thanks,' said Rudolph tonelessly, climbing out of the window. 'I'm going to need it.'

As Tony shut the storeroom door behind him, it occurred to him that he had not mentioned what was brewing up for Thursday. But it was probably just as well he had spared the little vampire this bad news on top of everything else. And anyway, there were still three more days to go . . . .

17
Uproar in the Passageway

Tony came home on Tuesday happily humming his favourite song, 'The good ship sailed on the alley-alley-o!' They had had their dictation given back at school, and Tony, who usually only got 4 or 5, had got 8 out of 10! That meant he would be given a book as a reward, and he already knew which one he would choose! *Vampire Tales for Advanced Readers*!

He swung the heavy entrance door open and went over to the lift. Then something made him stop still in his tracks: a shrill woman's voice and the excited yapping of a dog echoed up from the basement. Did it have anything to do with Rudolph, he wondered? He went over to the top of the stairs and listened.

'This must be it!' shrilled the woman's voice. 'This one 'ere. Just look at 'ow my Susie's fur's standin' on end!'

Then came a man's voice: 'That's Peasbody's store.'

'Peasbody?' echoed the woman. 'I caught their scamp of a son skulking round 'ere last night with a ruddy big bag. Furtive 'e was, and when I asked 'im where 'e was goin', 'e went red as a beetroot!'

'What lies!' hissed Tony to himself.

'What time was that?' asked the man.

'Would 'ave been about seven. I thought to meself then there was some funny business goin' on.'

'And since then you've noticed this—er—strange smell?'

'Oh no. *That's* been 'ere for nearly a week now.'

There followed a series of wild barks, and the woman squealed triumphantly. 'There you are! Look at my Susie! She thinks there's somethin' funny goin' on too!'

At that moment, the entrance door opened and Tony's mother walked in. 'What are you doing down here?' she asked in astonishment. 'Why aren't you upstairs?'

'Is that you, Mrs Peasbody?' called the woman's voice from downstairs.

'Yes. What is it?' replied Tony's mother.

'Would you mind coming down here for a moment?' asked the man's voice.

'What's all this about?' Tony's mother asked in a whisper.

'No idea!' he shrugged. He wasn't feeling at all well! He only hoped his mother did not have the storeroom key with her!

They went down the stairs. A dachshund with a bulging tummy came waddling over to meet them, barking furiously. It was Mrs Starling's overfed pet, Susie.

'I'm glad to see you've brought that good-for-nothin' son of yours with you!' Mrs Starling greeted them. She had lost her nylon scarf in all the excitement, and her rollers hung half-unravelled round her head.

'Did you call my son a good-for-nothing?' said Tony's mother in surprise.

'Only good-for-nothin's skulk around in the basement at seven o'clock at night carryin' 'uge great bags, to my mind!' countered Mrs Starling.

Tony's mother shot him a look which plainly said, 'I'll have words with you about this later', and said: 'I don't agree that you have the right to call my son names. I could call you a few, if it comes to that— you gossiping old woman!'

'What did you say?' snorted Mrs Starling. 'Gossiping old woman, am I? You, you . . .' and she searched for a suitable name to fling back.

'You must have misunderstood what I said,' smiled Tony's mother coolly. 'I said "one would never call you a gossiping old woman!"'

Mrs Starling was speechless.

The caretaker, who up till then had been standing silently next to Mrs Starling, now took the opportunity to come into the conversation. 'Mrs Starling has been complaining to me about the smell in the basement.'

'And what has that to do with me?' asked Tony's mother.

'She claims it's coming from your storeroom.'

'From *our* storeroom?' exclaimed Tony's mother. 'That's quite impossible. We clean ours out every two weeks! I've heard some wicked tittle-tattle from you in my time, Mrs Starling, but this is really too much!'

Mrs Starling had paled. 'What about my Susie?' she asked in a small voice. 'Why's she gettin' all worked up in front of your storeroom then?'

'How should I know?' Mrs Peasbody threw a withering look at the dog. 'Some dogs are always yapping at something!'

Tony felt as though a weight had dropped from

his heart. What luck Mum had stood up for him! Of course, she'd want to know what he'd been doing in the basement, but he'd think up a good excuse.

The wind had been completely taken out of Mrs Starling's sails, and even the caretaker seemed to find the whole business embarrassing.

'Please accept my apologies,' he said to Tony's mother, 'but you must understand, I have to follow up complaints of this nature.'

Mrs Starling swept her dachshund up in her arms and, without another word, she stamped off up the stairs.

'Come on, Tony,' said his mother. 'I bet you haven't had any tea yet.'

18
Happiness is a Plate of Spaghetti

'Now then,' said Tony's mother after she had sat Tony down at the kitchen table with a plate of steaming spaghetti in front of him. 'What were you up to in the basement at seven o'clock yesterday evening?'

With great concentration, Tony wove two strands of spaghetti onto his fork. 'It's a secret,' he said.

'Is it also a secret why you skipped gym yesterday?'

Tony looked up with a start. How had she found that out?

'Yes, you may well look surprised!' said Mum. 'I happened to meet Olly's mother who told me you'd been playing monopoly with Olly all yesterday evening.'

'Er, yes . . . well, you see, I didn't feel like going to gym yesterday. All that running round in circles, balancing on forms . . . .'

'But you always used to enjoy it so much?'

She was right.

'What about Olly? Didn't he feel like it either?'

Tony thought for a moment. She probably knew the truth already, so he said, 'Olly left the club six months ago.'

'So you were making up stories about your coach who had to go to the dentist?' Mum didn't sound too cross, in fact she sounded as though she was teasing. 'I would simply like to have an explanation for all this haunting in the basement?'

'Haunting? You shouldn't joke about things like that!' said Tony.

'Well, what *were* you doing in the cellar?'

Tony shook his head. 'It's a secret,' he repeated.

'I'm so curious,' said Mum. 'Couldn't you even tell me?'

'You'll find out on Thursday.'

'Do I have to wait that long?'

It appeared that she was treating the whole thing as a joke, which was of course the best thing that could happen. As long as she did not get suspicious, Rudolph was quite safe, and by Thursday he would have to be out of the basement for good, and he would be able to tell his mother that the secret had been that they had had a vampire down there as a guest for a whole week. Tony had to giggle when he thought of his parents' expressions when he told them.

'Eating spaghetti seems to make you laugh,' remarked his mother.

'Happiness is a plate of spaghetti,' Tony replied. 'Didn't you know?'

After tea, Tony went to his room and sat down at his desk. He opened a book and began his homework: How the Irish cut peat turves. But his thoughts kept returning to Rudolph in the basement, till finally he closed the book with a snap. Whatever else happened, he must speak to Rudolph today and make it clear to him that he couldn't stay in the basement any longer.

But what reason could he give his parents for going down to the basement again this evening?

What if he went down at about six, and then simply came up late for supper? Anyone can be delayed, can't they?

He opened his book once more. Even if he didn't know much about peat bogs, he was certainly good at making up excuses!

19
An Empty Stomach

'I'm just going out for a bit,' he said a little before six.

'O.K.,' said his mother, 'but don't forget: supper's at seven.'

Once downstairs, Tony took out his bicycle. An hour was a long time to wait, but he'd pass the time somehow—in any case, he had brought *Voices from the Vault* with him, and so he could at least read while it was still light.

He was back at the building by seven. Quietly, he opened the entrance door. There was nobody about, so he quickly picked up his bicycle and dragged it down the steps to the basement. The passageway was empty, and apart from the mouldering smell, which seemed to have grown stronger, all was as usual. He leaned his bike up against a wall and opened the door to the storeroom.

The little vampire was already awake. He was sitting up in his coffin, and by the light of a candle, he studied Tony with huge, hungry eyes. Then he recognised who it was, and his face took on a disappointed expression.

'Oh, it's you,' he said tonelessly.

His hair stood out wildly from his head, and his teeth clacked together furiously as if he had a shivering fit.

'Rudolph!' exclaimed Tony in a shocked voice. 'Are you ill?'

'Ill?' echoed the vampire, and tried to laugh. 'I'm just about to die of hunger!'

'Didn't you manage to—catch anything?' inquired Tony.

The moan which Rudolph gave as an answer made Tony's hair stand on end. 'Not even a mouse!' he groaned, and pressed his hands to his tummy. 'If only you knew how empty I feel!' He gazed at Tony with gleaming eyes, and ran his tongue slowly over his lips. Tony shivered: it suddenly occurred to him that Rudolph's eyes were fixed on his neck!

'Y—you wouldn't . . .' he began, and took a step backwards. Who could say what a starving vampire might not do!

But Rudolph shook his head and groaned even more loudly.

'Can you walk?' asked Tony sympathetically.

Rudolph got up and took a couple of faltering steps, then fell back in his coffin. 'If only I wasn't so dizzy,' he sobbed.

He looked so pathetic that Tony really did feel sorry for him. Was it fair to burden Rudolph with additional worries just now? He ought to have something to eat first. As always when he thought of what Rudolph liked to eat, a shiver ran down his spine, but he ignored it bravely and said: 'Perhaps I could help you?'

'How?' asked the vampire.

Tony hesitated. 'I'm not bad at catching rabbits,' he offered.

'Aren't you?' The vampire's face brightened. 'Well, we could give it a go!'

At once he jumped out of the coffin and went to the window. The prospect of food had made him feel much better. Tony rather regretted having offered to help.

'Er, Rudolph,' he began. 'About the basement—you see, Dad—and Grandpa . . . .'

But the vampire had already opened the window and clambered outside. 'Come on!' he called. 'There are two rabbits!'

20
Bad Luck

Tony followed him unhappily. Whenever it was a question of his, Tony's, interests, Rudolph always seemed to go deaf!

Now he was squatting on the lawn and looking around searchingly. 'There *were* two here,' he whispered.

'I think we ought to move,' said Tony, anxiously looking up at the lighted windows of the flats above, 'otherwise my parents might see us.'

'Where shall we go?' asked the little vampire excitedly.

'Er, over there,' said Tony, pointing to the playground which was shielded from inquisitive eyes by tall bushes.

'Are there rabbits over there?' asked Rudolph mistrustfully.

'Lots!' said Tony, although in fact he was not sure.

The two of them crept cautiously across the lawn. Tony did not relax until they were safely hidden in the bushes.

'Where are the rabbits then?' asked Rudolph, looking unenthusiastically at the climbing frames.

Tony pushed a couple of branches to one side. 'There!' he said. 'That's their favourite place.'

'Is it?' asked the vampire. His voice had become rougher, and his eyes gleamed. With a single bound, he vanished between the bushes, but was back almost immediately. His face was scratched and his cloak was even more torn. 'You call these rabbits?' he asked, holding out two fat spiders for Tony to see.

'Eeeugh!' exclaimed Tony. He could not bear spiders. He turned away quickly because he did not relish seeing how vampires tear spiders limb from limb!

But Rudolph plucked at his sleeve. 'You don't think I eat spiders?' he asked, and with a look of distaste, he let them drop to the ground. 'You've been watching too many bad vampire movies!'

'I was only thinking . . .' murmured Tony. Then suddenly he had an idea. 'I know! I could go to the hospital for you!'

'The hospital?' Rudolph was not impressed. 'What for?'

'They keep blood in jars there, I think.'

But the vampire would have nothing to do with it. 'I don't eat preserved food!' he said.

'I didn't know that.' Tony felt hurt.

At that moment, they heard footsteps approaching across the playground. At once Rudolph's expression changed. 'A human!' he whispered, and clicked his teeth together in excitement.

Tony jumped. Surely Rudolph would not really try to . . . . 'I th–thought we were after r–rabbits!' he stammered. 'A–and if you tr–try to catch anything else . . . .'

'What?' scowled the vampire.

'I'll—it'd be betrayal!'

The footsteps were now level with where they lay hidden. Rudolph had bared his needle-sharp teeth and was staring into the darkness of the bushes. His whole body quivered with excitement.

'No!' implored Tony.

The vampire turned on him in anger. 'Just you keep out of my business!' he hissed.

'I–if you try anything,' pleaded Tony, 'I–I won't be friends with you any more!'

The footsteps grew softer. A door opened and closed, then all was still. With a cry, Rudolph clapped his hand to his mouth. 'What an opportunity!' he wailed. 'I won't get one like that again.' Grinding his teeth, he turned on Tony. 'You call that helping? I'm starving, really starving. I'm going to do this hunting on my own!' He pulled his cloak around him determinedly and turned to go.

'What about the basement?' called Tony, but the vampire did not answer. Tony watched him vanish among the bushes.

Sadly he made his way home. He had made no progress, and now there was only Wednesday left!

'Do you call this seven o'clock?' demanded his mother as he came into the flat.

'No,' he muttered. The evening newsreel was already showing on the television.

'Why are you so late home?'

'I–I've been playing hide-and-seek.'

'For this long?'

'My hiding place was so good that no one found me till just now.'

It wasn't bad for an excuse, and Tony smiled in spite of himself.

'I don't think it's funny,' said his mother crossly.

'If it happens again, you won't be allowed downstairs any more in the evenings.'

I won't want to go, thought Tony to himself, as he turned to go to his room. At least, not after tomorrow.

21

Out Hunting

The clock on the church tower struck half past eight. Shivering, the little vampire made his way out from behind the trees where he had been lying hidden for the last half an hour. A couple of people had passed, but unfortunately not the right type: either they were in a pair, which made an ambush very difficult, or else they stank to high heaven of garlic.

However, a woman was now coming round the corner on her own. The little vampire quickly hid himself behind a notice board. Heels tapping, the woman came nearer. She was a tall, strong-looking woman, Rudolph noticed, and she would certainly not be short of blood! She had almost reached the notice board when she stopped. An ice-cold shiver ran down Rudolph's spine. Had she noticed him? Cautiously he peered round at the street. A few metres away, the woman was standing with her back to him. Her hair was held back with a slide, and her coat had only a narrow, flat collar, so that the vampire could easily see the pale expanse of her neck. He gave a low moan and, as if drawn by a magnetic force, he crooked his fingers and crept out from behind the notice board.

However, at that very moment, the woman called out: 'Rollo!' and clapped her hands. A huge alsatian dog came bounding round the corner, and the little vampire only just had time to spring back into hiding in the bushes. There he crouched while the alsatian snuffled around, and finally, as though the vampire

had not been through enough already, it cocked its leg against the bushes!

'Come along, Rollo!' said the woman. 'We're going home.'

The little vampire listened grimly to the sound of her receding footsteps. 'What a mess!' he grumbled, removing the thorns from his fingers. Although his tummy was growling with hunger, he did not move. It was rotten being a vampire, and he was not ashamed when two tears trickled slowly down his cheeks.

'Look, there's someone crying!' he suddenly heard a voice say.

'He looks so funny!' said a second voice.

'Yes, he looks like a vampire!' replied the first with a giggle.

In front of him stood two children, each one carrying a long stick, at the end of which dangled a brightly lit lantern. The little vampire quickly wiped a hand over his wet cheeks.

'What do you want?' he asked, shifting his stiff legs slightly.

The children were at the most eight years old—not very appetising morsels! But still, they'd be better than nothing . . . .

'Why don't you come along with me?' he suggested in his most friendly voice. 'I know a really dark path where your lanterns will shine much better!'

'Where is it?' asked the younger child.

'In the cemetery of course.'

'We'll have to ask our parents first,' said the elder

of the two.

'Why? It's much more fun without grown-ups,' said Rudolph persuasively.

'They're only just behind us,' said the child, and called back: 'Mummy, Daddy, come and have a look! We've found a real live . . .' but before he could finish, the vampire had vanished.

Rudolph ran to the wall of the cemetery without turning round once. He jumped over it and let himself fall to the ground with a sigh of relief. At least he was safe here!

As he looked around him, he was overcome with a feeling of homesickness, and he thought with longing of the happy times in the family vault. The yew tree and the entrance to it were not far away. What he would not give for a peep into his old home! He wondered whether the coffins were still where they used to be? Or had they been changed around since his banishment? Perhaps Anna slept next to Greg now.

Nothing much could happen if he took one quick look! He was sure that all the vampires would be out hunting at this time of night.

Then suddenly there was a rustling just behind him, and a figure in working overalls, with long wooden stakes poking out of the pockets, sprang forward. It was McRookery, the Nightwatchman, and he advanced upon Rudolph with a devilish grin.

'At last I've got you, you little rascal!' he said.

Nearer and nearer he came . . . .

'No!' cried Tony. 'No!'

He opened his eyes and found he was lying in his bed. Had he been dreaming?

'Tony?' he heard his mother's voice ask. 'What's the matter, dear?'

He switched on the light. His mother was sitting on the edge of his bed.

'Are you all right?' she asked.

'Yes,' he murmured. 'It was only a dream.' He shook his head.

'Sleep well then, love,' said his mother. 'We'll talk about it tomorrow if you like.'

22
Hefty Loads

After lunch the following day, Tony's mother said:
'You've been dreaming such terrible dreams lately,
Tony. A couple of times I've woken up, because
you've cried out in your sleep. And then you start
saying funny names like Aunt Dorothy and
Gruesome Gregory and Mabel the Mean . . . .'

Tony bit his lips. 'Do I really?' he asked
innocently.

'Yes.' Watching her son closely, Mrs Peasbody
said: 'I'm worried about it, Tony.'

So am I, was what Tony would have liked to reply,
but he could not admit it of course. So instead, as if
he hadn't a care in the world, he said, 'Oh, it's
nothing, Mum. Quite normal really.'

'Do you think so?' asked his mother doubtfully.
'Or do these terrible dreams have anything to do
with your nocturnal expeditions?'

'Wh–what do you m–mean?' stuttered Tony. Did
she know about his visit to the Vale of Doom?

'Well,' she began, 'it just so happens that recently
you've been staying out very late—once till almost
eight o'clock.'

'You're probably right,' admitted Tony.

'What do you do outside for all that time?'

'Play hide-and-seek, like I said.'

'Do you really expect me to believe that?'

He shrugged his shoulders.

'And what about this secret in the basement?' she
went on.

97

At once, Tony was on the alert. 'What about it?'

'Has it got anything to do with your nightmares?'

'No! Nothing at all!' said Tony quickly.

'Can I go down to the storeroom now?'

'Now?' asked Tony in horror. 'Why?'

'Because I want to find something in one of the old magazines.'

'Couldn't it wait until tomorrow?'

'I need to take the article into school tomorrow morning.'

Tony thought for a moment. 'I'll get it for you.'

'Would you really, dear?'

'Of course!' said Tony as though it were the most natural thing in the world.

'I don't know exactly which magazine it's in.'

'Don't you? Oh. Well, I'll bring them all up,' said Tony.

'Will you?' Tony's mother could not believe her ears. 'The whole pile?'

'Yes—why not?' said Tony. 'When do you want them?'

'Well, right now would be best.'

And so it happened that ten minutes later Tony could be seen taking the lift down to the basement. He had pretended all was fine to his mother, but in fact he could have screamed with frustration—and all because of the little vampire! He opened the storeroom door and turned on the light. The lid of the coffin was closed and from underneath he could hear a soft snoring. That's fine, thought Tony, you just sleep well! You've got me running round after you, after all! He would have given anything to take the vampire by the shoulders and give him a good shake, and let all his pent-up anger erupt in his face!

He stood still for a moment, undecided as to what to do. Perhaps he had better take a look at Rudolph. He had read that during the daytime, vampires sleep like the dead. Carefully, Tony took hold of the coffin lid and pushed it to one side. The head and shoulders of the vampire were now visible. Tony shuddered involuntarily. He had never seen Rudolph look so deathly! His eyes were staring glassily straight ahead, his cheeks had sunk in and only his mouth, sagging open slightly with marks of dried blood around it, showed that he was not dead after all.

'Rudolph?' he said quietly.

No answer.

'Rudolph?' he repeated.

The vampire did not move. The smell of decay hung pungently round him and nearly made Tony gag. 'Eeugh!' he said, and shut the coffin lid. Compared to that, Tony's feet even on their worst day smelled like a bunch of lilies of the valley!

He began to search for the magazines unenthusiastically. Finally he found them, neatly tied together, by the work bench. How many were in the pile? Fifty? Sixty? A hundred? He took the top ten. They were heavier than he had imagined. When he reached the storeroom door, he had to put them down in order to close it behind him. Then, arms aching, he lifted them once more.

'Here's the first ten!' he announced, as his mother opened the door of the flat.

'Oh, Tony,' she smiled. 'You're quite pink from all that effort! Are you sure you don't want me to help?'

Tony shook his head vehemently. 'It's good exercise!' he assured her hastily.

It took him six journeys back and forth before he managed to get the whole lot up to the flat. Then he fell on his bed, exhausted. His arms felt as if he'd been doing press-ups for a whole hour, and his knees felt like rubber.

'A friend in need is a friend indeed!' he said through clenched teeth. That was Gran's favourite saying, which he had often laughed about. Now he found it was just about true.

100

To try to take his mind off how irritated he felt, he took down *Voices from the Vault* from his bookshelf, but he had hardly turned a page before he fell fast asleep.

23
A Dangerous Plan

When Tony woke up, all was quiet in the flat. He looked at his watch: almost six o'clock. He must have been asleep for more than three hours! How could he, today of all days, when every minute counted!

He sprang out of bed and went to the door. At six o'clock, Mum was usually in the kitchen getting supper ready, but today all was quiet. There was no clink of cutlery, no music on the radio—had she gone out?

Quietly Tony opened his door. Even then, he still could not hear anything, so he made his way on tiptoes across the hallway. No one was there. On the kitchen table there was a note:

> Dear Tony, I've gone to meet Dad at the office. There's a little party going on there this evening. Give yourself supper, and be sure to be back in the flat by half past seven at the latest— we'll give you a call at eight o'clock. Love, Mum.

He let the note drop. A miracle had occurred! His parents would be out for the whole evening, and he could stay away for as long as it took to bring this matter to a close once and for all. He gave a little jump of satisfaction!

His tummy gave a gurgle, and he remembered that he had not had anything to eat. He cut himself a slice of bread and smeared it liberally with butter, then put a thick slice of cheese on top.

While he chewed, he thought feverishly of what

102

he should do. Go down to the basement and try to talk to Rudolph once more? He might listen this time. However, he soon discarded this plan. He had only to imagine Rudolph sitting yawning in his coffin, complaining how hungry he was, to realise he would have to think of a better solution!

What if he tried to find Anna? She would certainly sympathise with him, and help try to find a way out.

At the thought of Anna, Tony began to feel better. His plan had only one drawback: the only place he could be sure of meeting her was at the vault! He would have to lie in wait near the entrance until she came out . . . . He gave a shudder at the thought of all the other vampires who would certainly be coming out that way too, but it was a risk he would have to take! And just in case, he would hang his mother's silver chain with the crucifix around his neck, and put a couple of garlic cloves in his pocket.

He looked out of the kitchen window. It was still light, but soon it would be dusk and by then he must be at the cemetery. He took the necklace out of his mother's jewellery box, broke off four cloves of garlic, and left.

24
The Open Door

By the entrance door, Tony ran into Mrs Starling. She had her dachshund on a lead, and it began to bark loudly when it caught sight of Tony. She threw him a black look and walked stiffly past without responding to his greeting.

'Your dog used to be more polite!' he called after her, which only made the dachshund bark more frenziedly, and Mrs Starling dragged her, still protesting, into the hallway with an anxious look upwards at her neighbours' windows.

The world is in fact full of vampires, mused Tony, and the ones with pointed teeth aren't necessarily the worst kind!

Luckily he did not meet anybody else he knew, and so came without incident to the cemetery. It lay silent and deserted, and Tony was able to make his way undisturbed to the main pathway. Here the hedges were trimmed and the graves well cared-for, quite different from the other side of the cemetery where the vampires' vault was to be found. There was a fresh-looking grave by the side of the path, with flowers and crosses heaped on it, and Tony read the inscription: 'Alfred—you will always remain with us.' Tony grinned: what if Alfred turned into a vampire?

His laughter died away as he approached the chapel at the end of the path: its huge, iron-studded door stood open!

Tony stood rooted to the spot in horror. He

noticed how fast his heart was beating and he clutched involuntarily at the chain around his neck. Who or what was out and about in the chapel? While he debated whether to turn back or go on, a man came out of it, shut the door behind him and locked it with a large padlock. It was McRookery, the Nightwatchman. The long face, the large nose and the overalls with wooden stakes and a hammer poking out of the pockets could only belong to him! He knew well enough that the only way to get rid of vampires is to drive a wooden stake through their heart.

By now, McRookery had spied Tony. His face adopted a black expression and he came towards him with long, slow strides. It was like a bad dream, and Tony felt the sweat break out on his forehead. Any minute now, McRookery would lift the hammer and then . . . .

But instead, McRookery peered at him in an unfriendly fashion with his piggy eyes and said: 'What are you up to, my lad?' His breath smelt so strongly of garlic that Tony nearly held his nose!

'I–I was just passing through,' Tony stammered. He took a couple of steps backwards. 'I–It's my short cut home.'

'Is it now?' It was clear Mr McRookery did not believe a word of it. 'You're going the wrong way for the gate.'

He took one of the stakes out of his pocket and ran his thumb thoughtfully over its pointed end. Tony felt goosepimples rise on his skin.

'I'm on my way,' he said, turned round and ran off

down the main path all the way to the gate without stopping. Only then did he dare to turn round. McRookery was following him, but did not seem to be in any great hurry. In his hand he carried a large

ring of keys, and Tony supposed he was going to lock the main gate after him. Quickly Tony went through it and leaned against the wall on the other side, which here was smooth and newly painted. A pine tree hid him from McRookery's view and so he had a couple of minutes to catch his breath and think. It was already beginning to get dark—high time for him to be at the vault!

Since McRookery had barred the way through the graveyard, there was only one possibility left: he would have to climb over the wall at the back. Not a very pleasant prospect, because he might well meet a vampire coming over it the other way! And if he met a vampire before he had time to hide behind one of the gravestones near the entrance to the vault . . . he did not let himself think about that, so he ran till he reached the grey, crumbling bit of wall at the back of the cemetery. He looked quickly around on all sides and when he saw nothing suspicious, he took a foothold on a piece of wall and hoisted himself over the top.

25
The Vampires are Coming

This particular part of the cemetery had always given Tony the shivers: the grass grew knee-high, and overturned gravestones and twisted crosses gave the place an air of ghostliness. He was even more aware of it today than usual, and he looked anxiously over to the tall yew tree, under which the entrance to the vault lay hidden. Was there something moving over there? Tony's mouth felt dry, and he ducked swiftly behind one of the tombstones. His heart was beating so fast he thought it must be audible to the dark figure who now emerged from under the shadow of the yew tree.

It was a small, squat vampire, who looked around long and searchingly before finally spreading his arms under his cloak and flying away. Tony breathed a sigh of relief, because the vampire had looked hard in his direction more than once! There followed a second figure: a tall, strong-looking vampire who flew off without any hesitation. Could it have been Gruesome Gregory?

Then the stone at the vault's entrance grated a little, and Tony held his breath. A small, slender vampire, bent over a stick, came hobbling out of the shadows. Tony heard her groan softly. Then she hid her stick under the folds of her cloak and flew away. Was it Sabina the Sinister?

Once more, the branches of the yew tree moved gently and yet another figure came forward. It stood still and sniffed the air inquiringly. Tony's heart missed a beat: the figure was looking straight at him! Yes, there was no doubt about it, it had seen him! Now it was coming closer with swift strides—it was Aunt Dorothy! Tony was paralysed with fear. His whole body was trembling, and he stared straight back at her, unable to move a muscle. By now she was so close he could see her mouth, gaping wide.

'No!' he croaked in terror.

'Why ever not?' he heard Aunt Dorothy saying. 'It only hurts a little bit at first. After that, it's quite nice.' She reached out for him, and Tony could feel her cold, deathly breath.

'No!' he whispered.

'You mustn't struggle so, dearie,' said Aunt Dorothy. 'Otherwise I'll miss, and you'll get terrible scars!'

Tony thought he was about to faint. Suddenly, the stone at the vault's entrance scraped back once more, and a familiar clear voice called: 'Aunt Dorothy, what are you doing?'

Aunt Dorothy hesitated. 'What do you want?' she asked in surprise.

Tony opened his eyes and recognised Anna. A stab of relief shot through him. Perhaps all was not lost after all!

'Aunt Dorothy, you're wanted downstairs at once!' he heard Anna say.

'Downstairs, dearie? Why?' Aunt Dorothy was definitely distrustful.

'You're to be rewarded for finding out about Rudolph. But you must hurry up!'

Aunt Dorothy looked pleased and flattered, but

then her look changed to one of greed. 'What about him?' she asked, pointing at Tony.

'I'll keep an eye on him for you,' said Anna.

'All right then, dearie,' said Aunt Dorothy, casting one last longing look at Tony's neck before setting off towards the vault. 'You keep your hands off him, mind!' she called back over her shoulder, obviously forgetting that Anna only drank milk!

Once she had disappeared, Anna seized Tony by the arm. 'Come on, we must run!' she urged.

'What about Aunt Dorothy?' asked Tony, who was still numbed.

'That's the point!' urged Anna. 'She'll be back any minute, and if she finds you here . . . .' She said no more, but pulled Tony after her towards the wall of the cemetery. Tony followed as if in a dream. His head was swimming, and he still felt under the spell of Aunt Dorothy's eyes, which had taken away all power of thought or movement.

'We mustn't waste any time,' said Anna once they were safely over the wall. 'Aunt Dorothy can fly, and we've only got one cloak between us.'

'Wh–where shall we go?' asked Tony.

'As far away as possible,' said Anna, ''till Aunt Dorothy's given up looking for us!'

26
On the Run

'Why can't we hide?' asked Tony.

'Where?' said Anna.

'Back at my house?'

Anna shook her head. 'Aunt Dorothy knows where you live.'

'What about in the school then?'

'In your school?' Anna stopped still and looked at him. With great deliberation, she looked up at the sky and asked: 'And just how do you propose we are going to hide in there? Surely it's locked up?'

Tony grinned. 'It is,' he said. 'But my housekey fits the main entrance lock as well!'

'Does it indeed?' said Anna with a slow smile. 'I've always wanted to see what a school looks like from the inside.'

It was not long before they reached the school. In the small bungalow belonging to the caretaker a light was burning, but otherwise all was in darkness.

'I'll go first,' whispered Tony. He climbed over the wooden fence and Anna followed him. They crept across the school yard, which looked strange and unfamiliar in the darkness, and came to a long, low building. Tony pulled a bunch of keys out of his pocket, while Anna kept watch for Aunt Dorothy.

'Can you see her?' asked Tony anxiously.

'I don't know,' replied Anna. 'There's something moving over there, but whether it's Aunt Dorothy or not . . . .'

By now, Tony had the key in the lock and the door

opened. They quickly slipped inside and shut it behind them. Then they stood still and listened.

'Can you hear anything?' asked Tony.

'Yes,' answered Anna softly. 'There *is* something creeping around out there.'

Tony could not hear anything, but he came out in goosepimples.

'A–Aunt Dorothy?' he stammered.

'Perhaps.'

Several minutes passed, which seemed like an eternity to Tony. Finally Anna announced: 'She's gone.'

'Was it Aunt Dorothy?'

'Yes,' replied Anna. 'Didn't you hear her teeth clacking?'

At the thought that Aunt Dorothy was even now only a few metres away, Tony's hair stood on end. 'Do you think she knows we're in here?' he asked.

'I'm sure she doesn't,' Anna reassured him. 'Otherwise she wouldn't have gone away.'

Tony felt as though a weight had dropped from him. At last he'd be able to talk to Anna about Rudolph in peace.

27
In Tony's Classroom

However, Anna seemed to be interested in completely different things for the time being.

'Which is your form room?' she asked excitedly.

'The one on the left,' answered Tony.

She had already opened the door. 'Come on, Tony!' she called.

'You know, Anna, I must talk to you . . .' began Tony.

'Yes, yes,' she said carelessly. 'In a minute. Just now I'm much too inquisitive.' She ran round the room, counting the desks by the light of the moon.

'Thirty-five!' she exclaimed. 'How very sociable!'

'You call that sociable?' Tony was astonished. 'Do you think it's good that you only get attention once every lesson?'

'Of course it is!' said Anna. 'Then you can go to sleep for the rest of the time.'

'You'd get Zero for all your work!' retorted Tony.

Anna had stopped by the teacher's desk. 'Whose is this huge desk?' she asked.

'My teacher's,' answered Tony, who felt the inspection had already gone on for long enough.

'I see,' said Anna musingly. 'That's so she can frighten all the children, isn't it?' She bent down and looked in all the drawers. 'But she hasn't got any canes!' she said disappointedly.

'Canes aren't allowed any more,' explained Tony.

'Aren't they?' asked Anna. 'But Greg always

says . . . .'

'They have much better methods nowadays,' said Tony.

Anna thought for a moment. 'Rubber truncheons?' she asked.

'Marks.'

'Marks?' Anna did not understand. 'How do they work?'

'Very simple,' answered Tony. 'At school you get marks for everything. If you get good ones, you can go on to a "selective" school, as my parents call them, and later you'll get a good job and earn lots of money. But if you get bad marks . . . .'

'But that's unfair!' interrupted Anna. 'What if you can't help finding work difficult?'

'I know,' agreed Tony.

'What kind of marks do you get?'

'Middling.'

'Will you go on to a "selective" school?'

'Dunno. Depends if I want to,' replied Tony.

Anna looked thoughtfully out of the window. 'Perhaps it isn't so nice at school as I'd thought,' she said. Then something else occurred to her. 'Where's your desk?'

'This one,' said Tony pointing to a desk in the last row but one.

'Who sits next to you?' asked Anna. 'Not a—girl, I hope?'

Tony had to smile. 'No—a boy,' he reassured her.

Anna breathed a sigh of relief. 'Come and sit on your chair for a moment,' she said.

'Why?' asked Tony, sitting down.

'Because I'd like to sit next to you,' she smiled. 'Now it's as if we were school friends,' she said wistfully, sitting down next to him. 'I'd see you every morning in school, we could go to the playground together every day and in the evenings we'd do our homework together....' Her voice trailed off sadly, and she wiped her eyes with the back of her hand. 'Oh Tony,' she sighed, and turned her huge swimming eyes full onto him. Tony turned his head away quickly.

'I need to talk to you about Rudolph,' he said, to hide his embarrassment.

'Rudolph!' she exclaimed. 'You obviously don't find me very interesting.'

'No, it's not that,' Tony assured her hurriedly. Whatever happened, he mustn't annoy her! But how was he supposed to find the right words with Anna sobbing away, and he himself feeling so odd about it all?

'You see, Anna,' he began, 'it's about those slats of wood.'

'Slats of wood?' she asked.

'The ones in the basement. Grandpa's coming tomorrow, and he and Dad are going to go down and fetch it.'

'No!' exclaimed Anna. 'What about poor Rudolph? How can he get his coffin back to the vault in time? It's true that the ban has been lifted, but . . . .'

'Lifted?' Tony could hardly believe his ears. 'The ban's been lifted?' His voice nearly broke with relief.

'Yes—it was this morning,' said Anna.

'Well then'—words almost failed Tony—'he can go back to the vault tonight!'

'What about his coffin?' Anna reminded him. 'He won't be able to take that away by himself. In any case, he's bound to have gone out by now,' she added.

'We two could carry the coffin?' suggested Tony.

'What if Rudolph comes back and finds his coffin's vanished?' asked Anna.

'We'll leave a note on the basement window!' said

116

Tony. Anna was silent and looked away. 'Please, Anna,' he begged.

She looked sideways at him and gave a little smile. 'When you ask like that, how can I refuse?' she said.

Tony almost spread out his arms and gave her a hug, but he stopped himself just in time and gave her a friendly nudge instead. 'You're fantastic!' he said, and for once he meant it.

'Do you really think so?' she asked, and though there was only the light of the moon to see by, Tony realised she had turned a deep red.

'Anyhow,' she said, changing the subject. 'Someone in your form stinks!'

'Do you think so?' asked Tony. Apart from Anna's slightly musty smell, he had not noticed anything.

'Yes,' she said firmly, and her mouth turned down at the corners. 'A most revolting stink of—garlic!'

'Garlic?' echoed Tony. Then he suddenly remembered the pieces of garlic he had hidden in his pocket. Hesitantly, he delved in them and brought out the garlic.

Anna gave a shriek. 'No! Put them away! Do you want to kill me?'

'S–sorry,' stuttered Tony, 'I didn't realise . . . .'

'Don't you know the old vampire saying:

Beware of garlic! 'Tis so strong
'Twill give you cramps the whole day long!'

Anna had retreated to the other side of the desk. 'Quickly, get rid of the stuff!'

Tony opened the window and threw it out into the playground.

'I brought it in case I met Aunt Dorothy,' he explained.

'Do you really think it would have done any good?' asked Anna. 'It would just have made her more angry.'

Tony shuddered. 'What about this crucifix?' he asked, showing her the chain round his neck.

Anna dismissed it. 'Pure superstition. Only one thing helps, in fact.'

'What's that?'

'To be a vampire yourself!' said Anna, and giggled.

28
Painful Progress

On the way home, Tony said, 'I really can't believe the ban has been lifted!' It seemed like a miracle to him.

'At first it was to have been extended to four weeks,' explained Anna. 'My grandmother, Sabina the Sinister, was especially keen on that—as a warning to us other young vampires, as she thought. But when I told them all that Rudolph hadn't eaten for days, and was wandering around the place feeling sorry for himself, they began to be afraid that he might lie out in the sun one day in sheer despair, and expire—so they decided to let him come back to the vault.'

'Do you think he would have done that?' asked Tony worriedly. He thought of how weak and ill the little vampire had looked each time he went to see him. Perhaps he hadn't been taking the situation seriously enough!

However, Anna put his fears to rest. 'Don't worry,' she smiled, 'I always like to exaggerate!'

Tony looked at her sideways in astonishment. Without Anna... but surely, she must be in the same position as Rudolph?

'What about—I mean, you're in contact with humans as well?' he asked.

'Oh, they'd never catch me!' said Anna scornfully, and, linking her arm through Tony's, she added, 'It's nice of you to worry about me, all the same!'

Tony coughed to hide his embarrassment. He

wished Anna did not always show her feelings so openly! He carefully removed his arm from hers and said, 'We're nearly there.'

'Are your parents at home?' asked Anna.

'No,' Tony replied, 'and they won't be back before ten, that's for sure. But they're going to ring up at eight!' He suddenly remembered this, and looked at his watch in horror: it was already ten past eight!

'I must dash upstairs!' he said. 'Do you want to come too?'

'If I may,' laughed Anna.

They had hardly shut the front door of the flat behind them, when the telephone rang. It was Tony's mother.

'Hello, Mum!' said Tony, trying to speak normally even though his heart was hammering against his ribs. 'Where was I at eight o'clock?' He looked across at Anna, who was brushing her hair in front of the mirror in the hall. Why did she insist on standing within hearing distance? In any case, in all the vampire stories he had ever read, vampires weren't supposed to have a reflection!

'I was, er, on the loo,' he lied.

Anna laughed.

'Yes, of course I'm by myself, Mum. Who was that laughing? It was, er, someone on the radio.' He gestured frantically to Anna to go into the living room, but she stayed happily where she was and continued to brush her hair.

'Yes, Mum, I'm going straight to bed, Mum,' he said.

Anna laughed again.

'No!' said Tony emphatically into the receiver. 'There's no one here. It's a funny programme on the radio. Have I washed yet? Yes, Mum. Goodnight, Mum!'

Quite out of breath, he hung up. 'She nearly cottoned on to you!' he said to Anna reproachfully.

'I can't help it if you make me laugh!' she retorted. She put down the brush and turned around.

'Do I look pretty?' she asked.

'Ye–yes,' he stammered.

'Are you going to bed now?' she asked.

'No!' Tony growled.

'Pity!' she sighed. 'I'd have liked to have tried out

lying in your bed.' She looked at him hopefully, but Tony only blushed a deep crimson.

'We ought to go and get the coffin,' he said hastily.

'Already?' Anna sounded disappointed. 'You said your parents wouldn't be back till ten . . . .'

'They might come back earlier.'

'O.K.' She looked downcast. 'If you really think so.'

Tony gulped. Had he put his foot in it again?

'I—I've got a book for you,' he said to cheer her up. He went into his room and fetched *Voices from the Vault*. Giving it a last longing look, for he had only read half of it, he handed it to her.

'Thank you!' said Anna, sounding really pleased, and she put it into the folds of her cloak. 'Is it really for me?'

'Yes.'

'O.K. then, let's go and get that coffin!'

'Anna,' Tony began as they travelled down in the lift together. 'Is it true that vampires don't have a reflection?'

Anna looked ashamed and lowered her head. 'Do I look such a fright?' she asked.

'No, no,' Tony reassured her, 'I was just interested.'

'Vampires get such a rotten deal!' she complained. 'Not only do we have to sleep in worm-eaten old coffins, and wear these smelly old clothes, but we can't even look in a mirror when we want to smarten ourselves up a bit!'

Tony tended to agree with her, although he did

not say so out loud. He could imagine she would look very nice in jeans and a sweater, with her hair nicely brushed and a healthier colour in her cheeks . . . he was glad when the lift stopped, and he had to finish those thoughts!

'But you don't mind that I look like this, do you?' she asked shyly.

'O–of course not,' said Tony. It was just as well the lighting in the basement was so dim—he had gone pink again!

Tony opened the door to the basement passage and switched on the light. The smell of mould and decay was even stronger, and he had to smile when he thought of Mrs Starling and her sensitive nose! Soon she'd be able to breathe again!

'That's ours!' he said in a whisper, although they were quite alone.

'It stinks!' giggled Anna.

Tony opened the door and they went in. All was as before: the wood was up against the wall, and Rudolph's coffin was half hidden behind it, with its lid propped open.

'Not very cosy!' remarked Anna. 'And very lonely. Poor Rudolph!'

'What!' said Tony crossly. He had had a basinful of worries and problems since he had given the little vampire a home, and all Anna could say was, 'Poor Rudolph!' 'Perhaps I should have rolled out the red carpet for him?' he said sarcastically.

Anna laughed. 'No, no. But I was just thinking that for a vampire like Rudolph, who has always lain, er,—lived—, with other vampires . . . .'

'I suppose you think I should have come down here to live with him?' asked Tony cuttingly. He had torn one corner off a cardboard box, and on it he wrote in pencil this note for Rudolph:

Dear Rudolph—the ban has been lifted. We've taken your coffin back to the vault. Love, Tony.

Then he pushed the note between two of the bars on the window grating and shut the window from the inside.

'Are you cross?' asked Anna.

Tony only grunted.

'Tony,' she said softly, 'I only meant that I . . . well, if I had been Rudolph, I would much rather have slept upstairs with you.'

He did not answer, but began to clear away the wood.

'Can I help?' asked Anna.

'You could fix the lid back on the coffin.'

Together they lifted the lid. It was so heavy it made Tony's shoulders ache. He looked over at Anna worriedly. How on earth was he going to get both the coffin and the lid all the way to the vault? Anna was shorter than him by a head, and if he had difficulty . . . .

However, Anna smiled confidently, as though she had guessed his thoughts. 'I'm pretty strong,' she said, 'stronger than Rudolph.'

'Are you?' Tony did not believe her.

To prove it, she lifted the coffin from the middle. 'You see?'

'That's fantastic!' Tony was amazed. 'I'd never

have thought it.'

'No,' said Anna proudly.

She went to the foot of the coffin, Tony picked up the head, and carefully they carried it to the door.

29
Three on One Coffin

There was nobody to be seen, so they put down the coffin near the door and Tony locked it behind them. He suddenly felt rather queasy: what would happen if they met someone coming down to the basement, or on the way to the cemetery?

Anna broke into these thoughts with a whispered: 'Hurry up!' and they picked up the coffin once more.

Without turning on the light, they proceeded along the passageway and up the stairs. As all was still quiet by the time they reached the front door, they took the coffin outside and laid it down in the shadow of some bushes.

'Phew!' said Tony, rubbing his aching wrists.

'Not exhausted already, are you?' laughed Anna, who seemed as fresh as ever.

'No!' said Tony. 'Not at all!' He certainly would not admit it in front of her. 'Let's get on,' he said, and they set off again. They chose the unlit path across the playground, and reached the street without meeting anybody. Nearly all the cars were parked in their places and no one was to be seen.

'They're all watching telly, I'll bet,' said Tony.

'I know,' agreed Anna. 'While the evening shows are on, it's pointless for a vampire to go out hunting.'

'What do you do instead?' inquired Tony.

'We fly from house to house looking for a way in,' giggled Anna.

'Crikey!' said Tony, involuntarily feeling his neck. Just think how many times they left the window open at home! If Aunt Dorothy knew . . . .

'Shall we go on?' asked Anna.

Once again, they lifted the coffin and carried it along the pavement. Suddenly a figure emerged on the other side of the street. It was a man, and he was walking very unsteadily. He looked across at them curiously.

'Do you know him?' asked Anna.

Tony shook his head. 'He's drunk,' he explained.

The man tottered slowly across the street and came towards them. Tony's knees began to knock. Should they run off and leave the coffin? But then what would happen to it? The same thought seemed to have occurred to Anna, because she whispered: 'Let's just put it down and sit on it! Then he won't see it!'

She jumped onto the coffin and spread out her cloak, and Tony sat down next to her. By now, the man was close enough for Tony to smell the beer fumes on his breath. He sneezed.

'Well, children, move up a bit!' the man slurred. 'Make room for your ol' uncle—hic!'

Tony and Anna exchanged horrified glances.

'Or ishn't that a bench?' The man stooped down to examine the coffin more closely, lost his balance and toppled heavily against it.

'If I washn't so drunk, I'd shay that was a coffin!' The man peered at Tony and Anna through red-rimmed eyes. 'Ish that a bench, or isn't it a—hic—bench?' he asked.

'I–It's a bench!' stammered Tony.

'Well then!' The man sat down heavily and pulled

a bottle of beer out of his pocket. 'Cheersh!' he said, and took a gulp. Then he wiped the rim of the bottle with his thumb and offered it to Anna. 'Here! Have a drink!'

'No thanks,' said Anna.

'What about you, shunny?' he said to Tony. 'You'll have a shwig, surely?'

'I-I don't like b-beer!' stammered Tony.

'Don't like beer?' The man was amazed. 'Well, well. When I was a lad like you . . . .' He tilted back the bottle and took another long drink. 'You'll have one of these though, won't you—hic?' he added, and offered Tony a cigarette. Tony shook his head. 'Don't shmoke neither?' The man looked mystified. 'How'll you ever learn to, unlesh you have a go?'

'I don't want to learn how to,' Tony told him.

The man drained the bottle and flung it into a bush. Then, with trembling fingers, he tried to light his cigarette, and once this was accomplished, he leaned back contentedly—and fell over backwards with a crash! He looked so funny that Anna began to laugh.

'Ssssh!' hissed Tony. 'You mustn't make fun of drunk people. I think we'd better scram before he gets up!'

They picked up the coffin and raced off.

'Hey, wait!' the man called after them. 'You tricked me! That's no bench! Benches have backs!'

They saw him wobble to his feet with difficulty, and take a couple of faltering steps towards them, but they were already so far away that he did not try to follow them.

30
Mixed Feelings

'Will you drink beer when you grow up?' asked Anna.

'Certainly not as much as that man,' replied Tony.

'Why did he drink so much?'

'I suppose he had problems and wanted to forget them . . . .'

'Oh,' said Anna.

At last, they could see the cemetery wall jutting up in the darkness. Tony breathed a sigh of relief. His hands had lost practically all feeling, and his back ached. Anna, on the other hand, carried the coffin with an ease that looked as if she could have gone on all night.

'Just a little bit further,' she said encouragingly.

'Mmmm,' mumbled Tony.

They turned off down a narrow path. 'The best place to get the coffin over is here,' said Anna. Tony had mixed feelings. The thick bushes on either side of the path were an ideal hiding place—for Aunt Dorothy, for instance . . . . However, they reached the wall without incident, put down the coffin and Anna whispered: 'I'll go over first, and you can heave the coffin over to me.' She scrambled up and over the wall which was so high that Tony found he could only just reach the top by stretching up his arms.

'Why couldn't we have tried a bit nearer the vault?' he asked. 'It's much lower.'

'Too dangerous,' explained Anna. 'Think of McRookery.'

Tony looked helplessly from the coffin to the wall. They'd never do it!

'Ready!' called Anna.

Tony put his hands under the coffin and tried to lift it. 'I can't!' he said crossly.

'Try the lid first!' whispered Anna.

Tony took hold of the lid and heaved it with all his strength over the top of the wall.

'Have you got it?' he asked.

'No,' said Anna, but it was too late. Tony lost his grip and the lid fell with a crash down the other side. There was a sharp cry.

'Are you O.K.?' called Tony anxiously.

'No!' came the answer.

'Shall I come and help?'

'No!'

While Tony was thinking what he should do next, Anna climbed back laboriously over the wall. Her face was streaked with tears, and she held one foot out gingerly.

'Is it broken?' Tony was shocked.

'No,' she growled, and furiously picked up the rest of the coffin and heaved it onto the top of the wall. Tony watched her helplessly.

'Hold it there,' she ordered, and climbed over the wall herself.

'Shall I push?' he asked hesitantly.

'NO!' she said emphatically, and pulled the heavy coffin over with her. Tony heard her fit the lid on again.

'Are you cross?' he asked.

'Yes,' she said, and added bitterly: 'Butter fingers!'

'I didn't do it on purpose!'

There was no answer.

'Anna! I'm sorry! Please!'

Still no answer. Surely she hadn't gone off alone with the coffin? Tony put one foot on a stone and pulled himself up till he could just see over the top of the wall. Dimly, he could make out Anna carrying the coffin through the long grass. She stumbled, and he heard her moan softly.

'Anna!' he called. 'Don't go away! I didn't mean to hurt you.'

But she went on.

'Anna!' he called again, but she had disappeared into the trees.

Tony slid down from the wall and stood still, uncertain. Then he turned around and set off back home. It was funny—this time he never gave a thought to the bushes and the danger that might be lurking behind them. He kept seeing Anna, struggling through the grass with the coffin, and not turning round to look at him. It gave him a funny feeling in his tummy, as if he had eaten too many gooseberries and then drunk a pint of water. He stopped. Was this what it felt like to be in love? The other strange thing was that, although he should have been feeling heartily relieved to have got rid of the coffin at last, he didn't! All he did feel was that he had behaved like a bull in a china shop, and he didn't blame Anna for being so furious.

He reached the block of flats, took the lift upstairs and unlocked the door. No one was at home yet.

He fell onto his bed with a heavy heart. Will she ever forgive me? he thought, as he went to sleep.

31

All for Nothing

'Tony!' His mother's voice seemed to come from far away. 'Tony, get up!'

'Mmmm,' he mumbled.

'Tony, it's already quarter past seven!'

He rubbed his eyes and blinked. His mother had turned on the light, and it blinded him. All his limbs ached, and he groaned as he turned away.

'Are you ill?' his mother asked anxiously.

'Ill?' Now that was a good idea! And to be honest, he did not feel particularly well. He put on a woeful expression.

'I think I've got 'flu.'

''Flu?' His mother was concerned and felt his forehead. 'You don't feel as though you've got a temperature.'

'I ache all over,' he moaned.

'We'd better take your temperature then,' said his mother. She disappeared into the bathroom and came back with the thermometer.

'Here you are—and no funny business!'

'What do you mean, funny business?' asked Tony, sounding hurt. Nevertheless, his mother stayed sitting on the edge of his bed, and timed him with her watch.

'Tony, you aren't wearing your pyjamas!' she exclaimed suddenly.

'A-aren't I?' Tony was taken unawares, and he quickly drew the bedclothes up to his chin.

'No,' she said, gesturing to his chair. 'You've only

taken off your jumper and trousers . . . and what do your clothes smell of, anyway?' She held Tony's jumper suspiciously under her nose.

'Er, a little camp fire,' said Tony quickly.

'Camp fire?'

'Yes, we made one yesterday.'

Mum did not look convinced, but the three minutes were up, so she contented herself with taking the thermometer.

'98.5,' she said. 'Can't call that a temperature.'

'But I feel so rotten . . . .'

'Who's going to look after you if you stay at home?'

'Dad's here today, and so's Grandpa.'

'Dad? He left for the office a long time ago.'

'But he was going to . . .' said Tony, and stopped, puzzled. 'I thought he and Grandpa were going to work on the kitchen today?'

'They were. But something's come up.'

Tony felt his eyes fill with tears, and he had to bite his lip to keep from letting out a howl. He'd nearly killed himself trying to get the coffin out of the basement in time, and then when he did manage it, 'something comes up'! What a mean thing to happen!

'It's not that bad,' said his mother, smoothing back his hair. 'Everyone's ill from time to time.'

If only that were the problem, he thought, and turned his face to the wall with a sob.

'You can stay in bed for today, and I'll make you a cup of tea,' said his mother. 'But then I'll have to be going.'

When she had left the room, Tony lay in bed staring up at the ceiling. He really did have bad luck. On the other hand, at least the coffin was not in the basement any more, so he now had no need to worry when his parents announced they had to get something from the storeroom.

He sighed deeply once more, then crept under the bedclothes and, not very long after that, was fast asleep.

32
All is Revealed

When his mother came back at lunchtime, Tony was sitting up in bed. He had put a couple of extra pillows at his back, and was reading.

'Hello, Mum,' he smiled.

'You look much better!' she replied.

'Well, yes,' he said, a little shamefacedly. He would rather not admit that he had simply been dead tired.

'What's for lunch?' he asked. He was as hungry as a hunter after the exertions of the evening before.

'Potato pie,' answered his mother, 'but I'll have to go down to the basement to fetch the potatoes.'

'O.K.,' he said, and a feeling of great contentment stole over him: now it was all the same to him whether she went down to the basement or not. Suddenly he noticed she was looking at him in surprise.

'Don't you mind if I go down there?' she asked.

'No,' replied Tony. 'Why should I?'

She smiled. 'When I needed to search through all those old magazines down there, you wouldn't let me near the place. Has your secret disappeared then?'

'My secret?' Tony could not help smiling, although he tried hard. All he had to do now was explain everything to Mum. 'The vampire's moved out,' he said.

'The—what?' exclaimed Mum.

'The vampire who has been living in our

137

storeroom,' explained Tony.

'You and your vampires,' scolded his mother, shaking her head. 'Was it such a terrible secret that you now can't tell me the truth?'

'Don't you think that a vampire who has been banned from his family vault is a terrible enough secret?' retorted Tony.

'Vampires, vampires!' As always when this subject came up, his mother's voice became impatient. 'Can't you get interested in something more sensible?'

'Of course,' said Tony with a grin. 'Last week in the library, I chose a book on werewolves instead!'

'Tut!' clicked his mother crossly, and went out of the room. Tony laughed quietly to himself. As he had expected, she had not believed a word of it—luckily! He heard the front door close, and then it was a short time before the key turned in the lock once more. His mother came straight back into his bedroom. In her hand she carried a basket of potatoes—and the vampire's toothbrush!

'What is this?' she asked, examining the brush in obvious mystification. It was nearly bald, and the few bristles it did have were bent and stubby.

'I–er, don't know,' stuttered Tony. Sometimes it was easier to tell a fib!

'Eeugh!' said Mum, throwing it into the wastepaper basket. 'Someone must have pushed it under the door. And what a stink there is down there!' She took a potato out of the basket and smelt it. 'I hope the potatoes are all right.'

With these words, she went into the kitchen, and

Tony sprang out of bed and rescued the toothbrush from the scraps of paper in the wastepaper basket. He hid it under his pillow and leaned back contentedly.

'Will you call me when lunch is ready?' he said.

33

Nocturnal Gratitude

'Tomorrow, it's back to school for you,' said Mum firmly that evening.

'Mmm,' said Tony, hoping he sounded disappointed enough. His mother was not to be taken in, however.

'If you were really ill, you'd be asleep by now,' she pointed out.

Tony stole a glance at the clock. It was nearly eight! 'Yes, well I am a bit tired,' he said with an exaggerated yawn. In fact he was wide awake—understandably, since he had slept until lunch time! However, the best thing to do would be to go to his room and read until he felt sleepy. 'Goodnight,' he said.

'Night,' answered his father from the bathroom where he was busy hanging up shirts to dry.

'Sleep well, dear,' said his mother.

Once in his room, Tony pulled the curtains, put on his pyjamas and crept into bed. He thought longingly of the book about werewolves which he had described to his mother. That would have been just the thing to read tonight! However, unfortunately it still stood on the shelves of 'Adult Reading Material', which Tony was not yet allowed to take out of the library. What was more, he had given *Voices from the Vault* to Anna. The only thing left to do was to re-read one of his old books. He had just chosen *Twelve Chilling Vampire Tales* from his bookshelf when there came a gentle tapping on the window pane. Tony jumped in fright: Aunt Dorothy! After all, she did know where he lived . . . .

He tiptoed over to the window and peered through the crack between the curtains. On the window-sill sat the little vampire, smiling in a friendly sort of way.

'You?' Tony was surprised. He had thought of all the other vampires, Aunt Dorothy, Greg, Anna, but he had never thought it would be Rudolph. Rudolph had already had one banishment because of him!

'My parents are here,' he warned, opening the window and letting the little vampire in.

'What are they doing?' asked Rudolph.

'Watching the news on the television.'

'That's O.K.' The little vampire relaxed visibly. 'They won't bother us.'

'Aren't you scared that Aunt Dorothy will catch you again?' Tony asked.

'Yes, but I've come for Anna's sake this time.'

'Anna?' Tony felt himself redden.

'Yes. She said that whatever else I did, I must come and thank you.'

Tony's face went even more red. 'What for?' he asked.

'Well, because you've been so hospitable and let me stay in your basement . . . .'

'Oh, that!' Tony sighed with relief. For a moment he thought that Rudolph had come to try and sort out the quarrel he had had with Anna, but luckily the little vampire did not seem to know anything about it.

'It was nothing!' he said magnanimously. 'You'd

141

have done the same for me.'

'Yes,' the little vampire nodded eagerly. 'You can come and stay with me any time'—he paused—'but you'd have to turn into a vampire first!'

That gave Tony a fright. 'Vampire?' he exclaimed with a shudder, suddenly thinking that Rudolph's smile looked a bit menacing. 'I don't want to be a vampire!' he gulped.

'Don't you?' Rudolph paused again. 'Not even for —Anna?'

'No,' said Tony, trying to keep his voice from quavering. 'Anyway, we've quarrelled.'

'I know.'

'Did Anna tell you?'

'Yes. And she said I should ask you something.'

Tony blushed again.

'She asked me to ask you whether you were still mad at her.'

Tony nearly laughed out loud. Whether *he* was mad at *her*? 'No!' he laughed, and a great weight slipped from him. 'I'm not mad at her!'

'Really not?' asked Rudolph.

'No,' said Tony.

'That's good then,' said the little vampire and with these words, he went to the window and pulled back the curtains. There, in the far corner of the window recess, sat Anna, all wrapped up in her cloak.

'All's well,' explained Rudolph. 'You can come in, but keep it quiet.'

Gracefully Anna uncurled herself and slipped into the room.

142

'Hello, Tony!' she said.